WHUMP!

*... in which Bill falls
632 miles down
a manhole*

Susie Day was born in 1975 in Penarth, South Wales.
When she was seven, she promised herself that she would write
books for children, as grown-up books were all about dull things
like mortgages and tax discs. This promise was entirely forgotten,
until she saw an advert for the 2001 BBC Talent Children's Fiction
Prize in the Radio Times. She walked out of her front door, saw
an open manhole over the road, and started to wonder what
would happen if it went down, and down, and down...

The competition was judged by a panel including
Jacqueline Wilson and CBBC presenter Lizo Mzimba.
From over 4,500 entries, *Whump!* won first prize.

WHUMP!

*... in which Bill falls
632 miles down
a manhole*

by Susie Day

First published in 2004 by BBC Worldwide Limited
Woodlands, 80 Wood Lane, London W12 0TT
10 9 8 7 6 5 4 3 2 1
Text, design and illustrations © 2004 BBC Worldwide Limited

Printed in Great Britain

A catalogue reference for this book is available from the British Library
Cataloguing in Publication Data.

ISBN 0 563 49241 4

CONTENTS

For David, Siân, James and Tom

The Beginning

… in which beginnings are considered,
and discarded

At a quarter to four on a warm Tuesday afternoon, a ten-year-old boy ran at full speed around a corner, tripped over his extremely long stripy scarf, and fell 632 miles down a manhole.

That is *not* the beginning of this story. If we were to begin at the beginning, which is, after all, where stories usually begin, we'd have to start somewhere else.

We could wind the hands of the clock back a second or two, to see the ten-year-old boy (whose name, by the way, is Bill) risking a glance over his shoulder, and catching sight of the red and angry face of another ten-year-old boy not too far behind. That would explain why Bill was running quite so fast, and not really looking where he was going.

We could wind the hands back two or three hours more, to see the red-faced boy (whose name, by the way, is Paul, not that it matters) standing in the school dinner queue with carrot soup dripping down his neck. Since Bill was kneeling in a puddle of soup behind Paul, clutching an empty bowl and wearing a look of apologetic terror, it wouldn't be hard to guess how the soup got there. And since Bill began running for the school gates the instant the bell rang, before Paul had even *started* chasing him, we might presume that this sort of thing had happened to Bill before.

Understanding why Bill so often found himself running away from boys like Paul would probably snap the hands off the clock, we'd have to wind them back so far. We'd need to go back a year or two to see Bill's granny at the moment the speed-knitting craze hit the Sunnyglades retirement home; only then would we understand the eleven metre long scarf that covered half of Bill's face and trailed along the floor behind him, somehow making him look even shorter. To understand Bill's hair, which was long and blond and stuck out from his head in great curly springs, we'd have to go back another three years, to the day Bill's mother was told that you got most value out of a haircut when you had *all* your hair cut off. The resulting scalping revealed that Bill had the sort of ears that stuck out from his head, and made grown men point and laugh, and made babies cry. Bill vowed on that day never to go to the hairdresser's again. Bill's scarf, his unusual hair, and his general air of having the words "Good heavens, boy, what have you done *this* time?" shouted at him on a regular basis somehow made him the sort of boy people liked picking fights with - though he wasn't the sort of boy who won them very often.

But that still isn't the beginning of the story. We'd have to go back to the moment Bill's dad met Bill's mum for the first time, in the only all-night butcher's shop in a small coastal town in South Wales. For Bill's dad to get to that butcher's shop, we'd have to go back again, to the morning he saw the advert for the paperclip factory for sale, and decided that Wales might be the sort of place where people needed lots of paperclips.

And to get to the true beginning, we would still have to go back, to get to the person who invented manholes in the first place – not to mention the people who invented corners, Tuesdays, and going home from school at quarter to four. In fact, to get to the absolute proper beginning, we'd have to go back to a time long before anyone had invented pencils and paper, and since no one could write down what happened then, that is a story which is difficult to tell, and even harder to read.

The wise reader will have noticed that while we now know why Bill was not looking where he was going, who knitted his scarf, and how he and his parents came to be living in that small coastal town in South Wales, we still don't know what idiot left the cover off a manhole 632 miles deep.

But the answer to that is the end of the story, and since the beginning is already a muddle, we'd better save the end for later.

So, to recap: at a quarter to four on a warm Tuesday afternoon, a ten-year-old boy ran at full speed around a corner, tripped over his extremely long stripy scarf, and fell 632 miles down a manhole.

Chapter One

Falling Down

... in which good knitting is useful, and Bill
discovers how deep holes can be

You have probably never fallen down a manhole.
Don't feel too disappointed; generally people who fall
down holes of any kind get scraped and scuffed on the
way down, and there's always the unpleasant matter of
the splatting noise when they hit the bottom.

Falling was, however, something of a speciality of
Bill's. Falling off donkeys on the beach. Falling out of a
pedalo in the middle of a lake. Falling off his bike, and
his skateboard, and his rollerblades, and all those other
Christmas presents from his granny which made Bill's
father groan and roll his eyes when Bill unwrapped them.
If Bill could be said to have a gift, a genuine talent, it was
undoubtedly for falling. He was gold medal standard. But
even Bill was like a novice when it came to falling down
this particular manhole.

Speeding around the corner with one eye over his
shoulder, Bill's foot had tangled in the trailing end of his

scarf and, as he had pitched forwards, he had performed the usual drill. He put out his hands, scrunched up his eyes, and waited for impact.

It never came.

Instead, all he felt was a sudden coolness, as if the sun had gone behind a cloud, and a cold-fingered breeze ruffling his hair. It was very quiet.

Confused, Bill risked opening one eye, and saw... nothing. He stretched out a tentative hand, reaching blindly into the darkness and expecting at any moment to find the ground rushing up towards him, but all he could feel was a faint whisper of wind whizzing past his fingers. There was an earthy, mouldy smell, and a damp chill in the air.

While Bill was grateful not to have hit the pavement nose-first, he had a creeping suspicion that something quite extraordinarily bad might just have happened. Opening his eyes fully, he tucked in his knees and, like an astronaut, turned himself around in mid-air so he was falling with his feet pointing downwards. A cold blast of air billowed right up his trouser legs, but he did his best to ignore it, tipped his head back, and looked straight up.

High above, he could see two things: first, a circle of blue sky about the size of a dustbin lid, which was letting in a trickle of light; and second, by that light, the waving tail of his scarf streaming out above him, as if it were reaching up and trying to get out.

Bill breathed out a thankful sigh. If he could still see the mouth of the hole, then he couldn't have fallen that far. Maybe he could stop himself before he hit the bottom; maybe he could climb up; maybe Paul was already running to fetch help, and any moment now a rope would drop down to rescue him.

But even as he was thinking that that would be an uncharacteristically useful thing for Paul to do, the circle of light was getting smaller. Right before his eyes it was shrinking, disappearing, until the blue patch of sky was the size of a beach ball, then the size of a saucer, then the size of a boiled sweet, then the size of a full stop on a page.

Bill squeezed his eyes shut, and when he opened them again it didn't make any difference. It was utterly dark, so black he wasn't entirely sure which way was up, and the only sounds were the eerie whistle of air rushing past, and his own breathing, quick in his ears. Bill reached out, but he clutched at nothing until his fingernails scraped against the rough earth wall surrounding him and sent a shower of grit, gravel and dirt tumbling into the fathomless darkness below. He waited for the scattering noise as the gravel hit the bottom, but it didn't come. He was, he realized, falling down a bottomless hole, and someone so practised at falling as Bill knew that holes have bottoms. If this hole was bottomless, then it wasn't a hole; and if it wasn't a hole, then he was falling down some endless tunnel that he didn't even know the word for, and that was really rather terrifying.

Bill bit his lip, and closed his eyes again. And then he just fell.

And fell.

And fell.

He fell for so long, he got used to the chill wind

up his trouser legs, and the quiet, and the mouldy, muddy smell.

He fell for so long, he began to wonder if this was what the rest of his life would be like, nothing but falling and falling till he was old and wrinkly and his white beard grew upwards and filled his nose with hair.

He fell for so long that when he suddenly felt an odd tugging around his neck, he couldn't think for a moment what it was. Then his head began to spin, and his stomach got dizzy, and when he put out his hands to the muddy wall to try and slow himself down, it wasn't where it ought to be. As the tugging at his neck got tighter, Bill realized with a jolt that he was no longer just falling: he was *unwinding* down the hole, as the loops of his scarf unrolled themselves from around his neck. Somewhere up above, the trailing end of the scarf had got hooked on something sticking out from the hole wall, and now it was sending him spinning haphazardly downwards like a human yo-yo.

Away the loops came, stripe after stripe. The deep pink stripe made of stiff cottony wool that he'd never liked much. The pale blue fluffy stripe. The lumpy, bumpy orange stripe. It was still pitch black, but Bill didn't need to see; he knew every part of that scarf like each stripe was an old friend. The sea green with the flecks of white, the fuzzy grey, the pillarbox red. The one that could, in all honesty, only be described as the colour of stuff that comes out of your nose. On and on, stripe after stripe, with no two stripes the same, as his granny had proudly observed. She had found colours Bill had never heard of: vermilion, puce, cyan, burnt sienna, ultramarine.

She'd even invented a few of her own – termagant, and avuncular, and pipistrelle – and there were so many types and textures of wool that there could scarcely have been a sheep, goat or rabbit in the land without at least one bald spot.

Bill kept reaching up to try and catch himself, but up kept becoming down, and then sideways, before going back to being up, and just as he caught hold of the knitting it would twist away out of his grasp. He started to see bright flashes, and thought he must be about to faint. Then he caught a glimpse of scratchy gold wool whipping past his nose, and realized that while it was still incredibly dark, it was slightly less incredibly dark than it had been.

There was a light.

Appearing and disappearing as he pitched and rolled and spun downwards, but definitely there.

That's it, thought Bill, the bottom, I've found the bottom of the hole. Then he realized that the light wasn't just showing him the bottom of the hole. Tumbling past his eyes, he could now see the earthy wall around him, and attached to that wall were the rungs of a rusted iron ladder, snaking down towards the dim glow below.

Bill reached out every time the ladder spun into view. His jumper sleeve snagged on a corner, flaking off chunks of rust. His left little finger brushed past it, achingly close. And then both his hands closed around one slender metal rung, and, with a horrible wrench on his shoulders, he stopped dead.

Bill's feet searched out another rung below, and, gingerly, he stood up straight. There was an ominous creak, and several large clumps of dirt crumbled out of the wall, but the ladder held. The thick burgundy stripe of scarf around his neck went loose. Bill just stood there for a moment, clinging on gratefully and catching his breath. Once the world had stopped spinning, he could see the ladder more clearly. It was immensely long, obviously rather old, and not propped against the wall but fixed there with thick metal staples. It was also stretching up and down as far as the dim light would let him see, and he realized with embarrassment that it had probably been there the whole time, waiting for him to catch onto it.

As he stood there, a metallic tapping sound floated up from below, and he had the unnerving feeling that he was being watched. He peered down, and saw that the light below seemed brighter, and now that he could see better there was not one light but three; three individual beams of light, waving about and criss-crossing in the dark. The tapping sound went on, but now, above it, he could hear the faint murmur of conversation. The lights were talking.

Bill couldn't quite make out the words, but there seemed to be some kind of argument going on. One light, louder than the others, was saying the most, but every now and then it would be interrupted by a squeaky, cross-sounding light. The other light didn't say very much, and sounded rather bored.

Bill took a few careful steps down the ladder, unwinding a few more stripes of his scarf as he went, and leaned back so he could hear better.

"Nah, this place hasn't seen a Maintenance squad in years," said the loud light. "I'm telling you, Fray, you've got the map the wrong way up again."

"Have not!" said the squeaky light. "Tell him, Kit, tell him I haven't got it the wrong way up."

"Don't ask me," said the bored light. "Navigation. Not in my contract."

Bill frowned, and climbed down a little further, noticing that the rungs seemed to be getting thinner. The ladder let out a series of quivers and groans, sending more lumps of mud down towards the lights.

"See?" said the loud light. "I mean, look at this ladder. What cowboy put a 37-gauge sprocket into a loam and clay mixture like this? Probably fall right out of the wall the minute anyone set foot on it. And that's if it isn't rusted to pieces."

Bill swallowed nervously, and felt the worn rung under his foot begin to bend. He climbed down a few more rungs quickly, feeling his sweaty hands beginning to slip, but the ladder only protested more. When he stepped on the next rung, it snapped at once, and with a yelp he found himself hanging on for a moment just by his hands, as he scrabbled for a foothold. Feeling a unpleasantly familiar tug around his neck, he looked apprehensively down the hole, and was dazzled. All three lights were now pointing straight up at him.

"Um... hello?" called Bill, hearing his words echo into silence.

"Hah!" said Fray, the squeaky light, in triumph. "I told you, Varnish! That's a *live* one up there. Better call Retrieval to come and catch it."

Bill frowned, not sure if being caught by Retrieval was a good thing or not. But if he didn't get off that ladder pretty soon he wouldn't have time to find out. The rung he was standing on was creaking worryingly. He was going to have to come up with a Plan.

Moving as quickly as he dared, Bill began to unwind the remaining loops of scarf from around his neck. Cherry red. Bottle green. Magenta, turquoise, electric blue shot through with silver thread. Yards of wool unfurled down the hole, till the whole scarf, right down to the lumpy mud brown stripe at the end, was dangling free.

Shivering, as his neck felt the cold for the first time in some years, Bill gave the scarf a quick yank to test it, and then – holding his breath, because this was the part of the Plan he was least keen on – grabbed the nearest stripe, and let go of the ladder. He swung out into the gloom, wincing as thousands of tiny knots took the strain. The wool stretched and complained, lowering him centimetre by centimetre. Alongside him the ladder moaned and shuddered, sending more grit downwards. But nothing unravelled. Whatever the scarf was hooked on didn't break.

"What's it doing?" asked Kit, in a noisy whisper.

"Looks like it's climbing down that big bit of string," hissed Varnish.

Bill looked at the fat, cushiony purple stripe in his hands as it slowly slid out of his grasp, and thought that this was a rather generous description. The Plan had seemed simple enough while he was Planning it: all he had to do was hold on to the scarf with his hands and feet, like the ropes in PE lessons, and climb down to the bottom. Now that he was actually doing it, he was noticing a number of small, but rather important, flaws.

The first problem was that Bill wasn't very good at holding onto ropes in PE lessons. Bill wasn't very good at anything in PE lessons, and that was without having sore hands and aching shoulders and a rather giddy stomach. Now that he was clinging onto a bobbly stripe of cornflower blue and slipping inexorably down towards a grubby mayonnaise-coloured one, he realized that since he'd never managed to climb up the ropes in school, he was a complete beginner at climbing down them.

The second problem was that while Bill was slowly but surely slipping down the hole, it appeared that the bottom of the hole was coming up to meet him, and now that it was closer, he could see that it wasn't the bottom at all. The three beams of light were slowly rising up the wall towards him, tapping as they went, and in the dim light Bill could see three pairs of hands. Wrinkled hands, with long, pointed fingernails. Fingernails that, now that he thought about it, looked a lot like claws.

As they drew closer, Bill saw that hanging from harnesses pegged into the wall of the hole, not too far below his feet, were three small figures. They seemed to be climbing up the wall by pegging themselves onto it, like rock climbers. He couldn't see them too clearly; their matching yellow boiler suits were so strung about with pockets, tool belts and coils of rope that it was hard to make out their shape, and the shafts of light, which were coming from lamps on their hard hats, dazzled him. But he got the strong impression that the faces below the lights were rather hairy and pointed, with prominent teeth, and he caught a glimpse of something thin trailing down the wall behind each of them which looked suspiciously like a tail.

"Excuse me," said Bill nervously, feeling slightly ridiculous, but wondering just how far the hole carried on below the lights. "Do you think you could help me?"

The tapping stopped.

"Help?" said Kit, slowly. "Do we do Help?"

"Don't know about that," said Varnish, sounding doubtful. "We're Maintenance, mate, not Help."

"It is rather urgent," said Bill apologetically, sliding down to the black stripe just above their hard hats, and noticing that one of the rats was holding a small metal box, which was extending a thin strip of silver up the hole alongside him. He shrank back as the strip came to a level with his face, and with a whirr, halted.

"What are you doing, Fray?" said Varnish, sounding alarmed.

Now that Bill could see it up close, the silver strip looked rather like one of those springy tape measures carpenters use, except that instead of numbers, the measurements were all in words, in print so small he had to squint to read it. At the top were tiny things, like Germ, and Spiderweb, and Eyelash. Somewhere by his nose it read Gerbil; by his chin was written Telephone. And in between these, there were hundreds of other words he didn't recognize - Frowler, which was about the same size as a Crinkle-Cut Chip, and Patoosh, which was somewhere between a Rugby Ball and a Hubcap, and Scrinty, which seemed to be the smallest thing there was.

"You never know. It might be... you know...

important," said Fray, giving Bill a disturbingly toothy smile.

Bill bit his lip, sure that he wouldn't be. His eyes travelled down the list of strange measurements, and just as they skimmed over Chimpanzee, the tape gave a click, and with a whirr retreated back down the hole.

There was a long pause.

"Well, that's that," said Kit, flatly.

"Too short," said Varnish.

"Ever so much too short," said Fray, sounding disappointed.

Bill felt his cheeks going pink as his sweaty hands let two more stripes slide past, and thought to himself that while he wasn't the tallest of people, being called short by a rat, even a giant mountaineering rat, was a bit much. Then he realized the biggest rat was looking up at him with suspicion.

"Here," Varnish said, in a loud whisper. "What if he's a... a..." He began winking and pulling faces suggestively.

"Contortionist?" suggested Fray.

"Person with something in his eye?" said Kit.

Varnish shook his head.

"No," he hissed. "What if he's an Ess Pee Why?"

"A spy?" said Bill, quite loudly because he was so surprised.

The three lights all turned on him, and he screwed up his eyes as he felt more wool slip between his fingers. When he opened them again, he was dangling somewhere below their boots.

"I'm not a spy," said Bill quickly, feeling panic begin to

rise. "Really, I'm not. I've never even met one."

The three beams of light turned away from him, criss-crossed one another up above for a moment, then gazed back down on him.

"*Definitely* a spy," said all three voices, now sounding a little distant.

"We can't just let him fall," said Varnish.

Phew, thought Bill.

"We have to *help* him fall," said Varnish.

Looking up, Bill saw Varnish delve into one of his bulging pockets, and pull out the largest, shiniest pair of scissors Bill had ever seen. They glinted for a second in the lamplight, and then flashed, and Bill heard a loud snip.

And he was falling again…

Falling…

And falling…

And falling…

Until, at last, he hit the bottom.

Chapter Two

At the Bottom

… in which friends are made

WHUMP!

That was the noise that Bill made when he hit the bottom. Not splat, or crunch, or splinter-splinter-ouch-splinter-ouch, but a stately huffing sound, like a pebble dropped into a bucket of wet sand.

Bill lay quiet for a moment and waited for the spinning in his head (not to mention the churning in his stomach) to stop. Then he opened his eyes.

He appeared to be lying on a heap of feathers at the bottom of a well. Dimly, he could make out four walls of rough stone blocks covered in something slimy, and there was the sound of water dripping. His scarf, which despite being snipped in half was still extremely long, was lying in a bundle on his lap. Otherwise he could see very little, having sunk deep into the heap. The feathers tickled his face, and he reached out to pick up a handful.

Not feathers. Paper. Thousands of pieces of torn paper, as if years' worth of out of date phone books, dog-chewed newspapers, and unsent Valentine's Day cards had been ripped to shreds and dropped down the hole before him to break his fall. Bill peered at the scraps he was clutching. A few were brightly coloured, but most of them were the sort of stiff, heavy paper, slightly yellowed, that you found in old books. Some even had printing on them.

Sitting up awkwardly to get a closer look at the words, Bill felt the pile of paper shift under him, and realized with alarm that the heap was more like a tower, and not a very solid one. The mound of scraps tilted to one side, steadied encouragingly for a moment, then tumbled away from under him, sending him plunging downwards in a flurry of paper. His head hit the floor with a resounding thud, and everything went very, very black.

When he woke up again, he was lying flat on his back on what felt like a very firm bed. A cosy blanket seemed to be covering his chest, and a hum of gentle female voices murmured soothingly. Someone was wiping his face with a warm cloth. As bottoms of holes went, Bill thought, this one wasn't so bad.

Except, of course, for a thumping great headache. And the funny smell, like wet dog and sawdust mixed up with mouldy teabags. The cloth that was washing his face could have been softer. And under the mellow humming voices, he could hear what sounded like two quite grumpy people having an argument.

"I didn't say he *was* one, I said he might be," said a cross-sounding girl's voice.

"You think so?" answered a deeper man's voice, with a pompous tone. "It wasn't the most regal of entrances."

"Yeah? You want to know how dignified *you* looked

when you landed on your face?" snapped the girl.

"Shhh," chorused the female voices, speaking all at once. "I'm sure he'll be lovely, whatever he is."

"Nah, I don't think he is one," sighed the girl, sounding fed up. "I've met plenty, and none of them looked like him."

Bill wondered what exactly he wasn't, and then wondered whether him not being it was something he should be worried about.

"I'm sure he'll wake up soon and tell us all about it," the humming voices continued. "Unless he's already dead," they added, in the same cheery tones.

"You don't think he really is dead, do you?" said the man, anxiously.

"I hope not," said the cross girl. "There's nowhere to put a dead body in here. We'd keep tripping over him."

"And I can't include him in the log if we don't know what he is," agreed the man. "Although I suppose I could always dissect him, and see if his insides look familiar."

Bill decided that this might be a good time to wake up and introduce himself.

Then he opened his eyes, and started to wonder if perhaps the melodic voices had had the right idea, because if he wasn't dead, he certainly wasn't very well.

Instead of a roomful of humming women and grumpy people, he could see nothing but the rather blurry image of an antelope sitting on his chest, its velvety nose quivering a couple of centimetres from his own.

Bill blinked, and wondered if this was his own strange version of the little birds that fly around people's heads on cartoons after they've been knocked on the head. But the antelope didn't disappear. It simply sat there, a small brown deer-like creature, with two pointy horns on its head, and big shiny eyes like melted chocolate. In fact, Bill thought, it looked quite sweet. Then the antelope leaned even closer and gave his face a long, friendly lick with its little pink tongue, and Bill realized what the warm but scratchy cloth that had been bathing his face had been, and decided perhaps it wasn't quite so sweet after all.

Screwing up his face, he started wiping it with his sleeve, but the antelope's expression stopped him. The creature looked suddenly quite sad, or disappointed, or both, as if it had hoped Bill might have remembered its birthday this year, but wasn't all that surprised to learn that he hadn't.

"I... I'm sorry," said Bill, haltingly. "I didn't mean to hurt your feelings."

The antelope blinked at him.

"I mean... it was very kind of you to lick my face," he added, uncertainly.

The antelope blinked again, unmoving.

Unnerved by the silence, Bill rolled his head to one side to look about him. With only two bare light-bulbs giving off a sickly yellow glow, most of the room was lost in shadow. He could make out the mountain of torn paper in the middle of the floor, under a large black hole in the ceiling, and an iron door with a very cobwebby keyhole. And in the shadows were three of the oddest-looking people he'd ever seen.

There was a scruffy girl who Bill guessed was two or three years older than him. She had bright blue eyes, and a nose with a smudge on it peering out from under a knotty mess of dark hair. Her short dress was equally grubby, and was teamed, rather unexpectedly, with a pair of khaki army trousers and some heavy black boots.

Towering over her was what looked like a tall thin bald man, if tall thin bald men had damp, mottled skin the colour of old chewing gum, thin fishy lips that turned downwards, and jelly-like yellow eyes. Although his shoulders were broad, the head on top was tiny and wrinkled, like a walnut. He was dressed in a pair of bright orange dungarees which were slightly too short, and had some sort of circular shiny symbol embroidered on the front pocket.

By the grey man's knee stood a fuzzy green thing, about a metre tall, with a head shaped like a squirrel's. She (at least, he thought it must be a she) had enormous dark almond eyes, which sparkled like pebbles rubbed smooth by a stream, and were framed by long soft lashes. A row of tiny silver hoops dangled along the length of her tufty squirrelish ears, and she wore flowing mossy green robes, with tinkling silver fringes edging the full sleeves.

"Is he talking to the *antelope*?" said the scruffy girl, wrinkling up her nose incredulously.

Bill blushed, suddenly feeling rather ridiculous.

The grey man shook his head, pursing his fishy lips. "Obviously one of the lesser species," he said.

"Ooh, he has the gift of animal speech!" sang the fuzzy green thing, bounding out of the shadows excitedly. The room filled with voices as she spoke. Bill looked round for the other people, but there was no one else there.

"Tell me, lovely antelope," said the green thing, reaching out a small fuzzy paw to stroke its ears, and setting the chimes on her sleeves jingling. "Are you happy? Where did you come from? What happens in your dreams?" The voices rang out again, and Bill realized that they were all coming from that one small green thing.

She looked expectantly at Bill, waiting for his translation. The antelope blinked unhelpfully, and licked his face again.

"I don't really…" Bill began, apologetically.

"They are quite personal questions," sang the green thing, nodding her head as if agreeing with him. "You should probably get to know it better first."

"Oh, enough!" shouted the scruffy girl, pushing the green thing aside. "It's an antelope. It's probably happy because it's too stupid to be anything else. It came from that big hole up there, just like you did. And in its dreams, it probably goes to somewhere warm and sunny and very far away, where there aren't any irritating little elphs asking it stupid questions which it can't answer because it can't talk!"

All eyes turned to the antelope, which might well have been thinking it could talk perfectly well to other antelopes, which was more than enough for it. Alternatively, it could just have been thinking about how nice leaves are, or who would win the football. Antelopes are enigmatic creatures; what goes on inside their heads, only they know.

Whether it had understood or not, this antelope had evidently decided it was bored of being Bill's blanket. Standing up carefully on its four spindly legs, it hopped off his chest, trotted over to the paper mountain, and curled up among the soft scraps, closing its eyes. Within moments it was snoring gently.

"Now," the scruffy girl continued loudly, "shut up and let me ask my question."

She took a step forwards, vainly tried to damp down her wildly tangled hair, and gave Bill a forced, uneven smile which was ever so slightly frightening. Smoothing down the front of her tatty, dusty dress, and granting him a glimpse of fingernails so dirty you could grow peaches under them, she dipped into a clumsy curtsey, then chanted out, in the sing-song voice used by people who answer the phone too often:

"His royal majesty and most gracious sovereign the forty-fifth King of the province of the many monarchs does hereby present in absentia but before all witnesses his youngest and only daughter the Princess Tallulah von Stuffelheim, and henceforth demands that any and all of noble bearing and high birth here present do make themselves and their marital intentions known forthwith."

She looked at Bill expectantly. "Well?" she said, her hands on her hips.

Bill gingerly sat up, and rubbed the sore spot on the back of his head.

"Um… sorry," he said, trying to ignore the grey man, who was now crouching on the floor beside him, prodding his arm with a long bony finger and staring at him with an expression of mild distaste. "Could you say that again?"

She sighed heavily, then fixed the grin onto her face, bobbed into another curtsey, and rattled through the speech again, this time even faster. Most of it still whizzed over Bill's head, but there was one word that had stuck out both times.

"You?" he said. "You're a princess?"

"Yeah," she said, hands on hips again and sounding dangerous. "The Princess Tallulah. You got a problem with that?"

Bill took another look at her fierce face and tatty clothes, and realized that the faded dress had probably once been pink and frilly, and that the knotty dark hair would probably comb out to a princessly smoothness. In fact, he could even see the glint of a small, tarnished crown, buried somewhere in all the tangles.

Bill realized he was staring rudely, and shook his head. "No, no of course not. It's just that… well, where I come from, princesses don't really look like you."

"Where I come from, handsome princes don't really look like you either, matey, but we can't all be picky. So come on, spill. Are you of noble blood and royal parentage?"

Bill yelped as the grey man pulled off his left shoe and tickled the bottom of his foot experimentally. The man looked startled, then mumbled something to himself and nodded, as if taking notes. Then he handed Bill back his shoe and leaned over Bill's face, jabbing at his neck, waggling his jaw, and tentatively sniffing a curly spring of hair.

"Um," said Bill, distracted. "I don't think so. My parents mfffff…"

Here he broke off, as the man reached into his mouth and grabbed his tongue, tugging at it gently to see how it was attached. Then he let go, and began investigating Bill's ear.

"My parents," Bill began again with a cough, "are just ordinary people."

"So you're not a handsome prince, then?"

Bill eyed her warily, and shook his head as best he could with the grey man's long clammy fingers pinching his ears.

"No uncles and aunts on thrones anywhere? Not even a second cousin twice removed living in a teensy-weensy castle?"

Bill shook his head again.

"Thank goodness for that," said Tallulah, breaking into a broad, crooked smile. "Now I won't have to marry you. This place is depressing enough without having to put up with a husband."

Bill smiled politely, and then squeaked, as a curious grey finger unexpectedly poked up his left nostril.

"Hey! Pick your own nose," said the princess, nudging the man's shoulder with the toe of her boot.

Bill looked up at the mottled face and noticed that the man didn't actually have one. There was a smooth bump in the moist grey skin where a nose would be on most people, but nothing you could breathe through. In fact, now he was looking, he could see the man seemed to breathe through a series of narrow slits, like gills, which nestled just below his ears.

"Sorry," said Bill, realising he was staring.

The man gave him a thin-lipped smile, then removed the finger from Bill's nose, frowned at it, and delicately wiped it on the green thing's back. She didn't seem to notice, and tinkled over to give Bill a twinkly smile.

"So, lovely new person, we must introduce ourselves, too. I'm Phly, an elph of the greenlands, and our long-fingered friend from far beyond the outer skies is named Whistler."

At this, the grey man straightened up to his full height, cleared his throat pointedly, and gave Phly a stern look.

"Thank you, Phly, but I can handle my own introduction," he said, turning to Bill. "Don't mind my green colleague, she's apt to confuse matters. My name, in full, is Engleburton Hartdegen Shelmerdine Hikaru..."

Bill kept expecting the grey man to pause for breath, but he went on speaking, rocking back on his heels and staring straight ahead with a slightly glazed look in his yellow eyes.

"... Sebastian Ludovico Maldis Rotblat..."

Tallulah and Phly seemed unconcerned, as if they'd heard it all before. After several minutes, he finally seemed to be slowing down.

"... Eustace Mandeville Wetenhall Kropotkin-Jones."

Whistler breathed noisily in through his gills, and smiled proudly at Bill. "I was named after my father," he beamed.

"That's nice," said Bill slowly, thinking how much it wasn't.

Whistler sighed. "Unfortunately, since some lesser beings," (here he paused and glared at Tallulah and Phly) "seem to struggle with my full title, it is logical while I'm among you to find a suitable, shorter name. Might I suggest 'Captain'?"

Bill nodded at Whistler seriously, trying to ignore the giggling fit that seemed to have enveloped Tallulah.

"Of course, on my home planet, they call me 'my lord', but I'm not one to stand on ceremony," he added. "I'm quite well-travelled for a Quxynggrotly. Perhaps you've heard of me?"

Bill shook his head, not trusting himself to open his mouth while Tallulah's infectious giggling continued. Whistler glowered at her, emitting a faint whistle through his gills.

"Oh, don't get your dungarees in a knot,"Tallulah said through her laughter. "Whistler's a very nice name that suits you down to the ground. And you're a plain old ordinary alien, not a Quxynggrotly. You only made that up so you could beat me at Scrabble."

"You play Scrabble?" said Bill, and then wondered why this one fact seemed more bizarre than small green squirrelly people, or aliens, or grubby princesses wanting to marry him.

"Yeah. Stuff falls down the hole all the time," said Tallulah.

"Lovely presents!" sang Phly.

"A lot of useless rubbish," said Whistler, nodding towards a shadowy corner, where a dark pile of things was just visible. Bill could make out the outline of a broken canoe paddle, a bent pram wheel, and the wiry skeleton of an old lampshade. It certainly looked more like a rubbish dump than anything you might find under the Christmas tree.

"So," Phly hummed, clapping her hands together and kneeling close to him. "What should we call you?"

"I'm Bill," said Bill.

"Bill," the three of them repeated. Phly sang the word

over and over, with different notes chiming in, as if testing out which tune was right for him. Whistler mouthed it to himself silently, looking unimpressed. Tallulah chewed the inside of her cheek thoughtfully.

"A bit short," she said eventually, "but I've heard worse."

"And tell us, *Bill*," Phly said, emphasising his name with a sweet harmony that sent a tingle up Bill's spine, "what kind of a thing are you?"

"Aha!" said Whistler, striding forward and holding up a grey palm. "Stop. I'll answer that one. After close and careful examination, and using the capacious quantities of information I've amassed on my many daring and dangerous travels, I'm in no doubt that our new colleague is from the twilit lowlands of level 29."

Whistler knelt behind Bill and took hold of his head. "The pale complexion comes from skulking in the darkness in search of carrion. These unusual head attachments" (and here he took hold of a curly spring of hair) "are presumably some kind of tribal marker. Bill here is, without a doubt, a mature example of Antenmann's Trigg, a species first identified by Gregorius Antenmann on the second voyage of his fine ship the Brian IV, and widely believed to have died out around 700 years ago."

"Oh, how exciting!" trilled Phly, clapping her hands.

"He doesn't look very skulky," said Tallulah doubtfully.

"All part of their cleverness," said Whistler, sagely. "In Antenmann's time the Trigg were so good at lurking in dark places, they kept losing each other. Probably why they died out. Fortunately for Bill here, evolution has sorted out that little problem, eh, Bill?"

Whistler tousled Bill's hair and smiled proudly.

"Um," said Bill. "Actually, I'm not a Trigg."

Whistler stared at him in a not altogether friendly way.

"Are you sure?" he said.

Bill nodded guiltily.

"We'll let the Knowletron sort this out," muttered Whistler, rootling in the pocket of his dungarees. He produced a small folded square of silver, and opened it out flat on his palm, before tapping the centre. A transparent globe of coloured lights that twisted and danced appeared above the square, hovering in the air. Whistler jabbed a bony finger into the globe, and the image changed, the sphere spinning and scrolling through what looked like numbers and letters, punctuated by the occasional picture of a three-headed kitten, or a tree with ears for leaves. Whistler kept his finger moving, spinning the globe faster, then brought it to a sudden halt and reversed the spin for a turn or two. He stared hard at the image, then looked at Bill.

"Just the two eyes?" he said, suspiciously.

Bill nodded.

"Oh, bother," said Whistler, snapping the square shut and slipping it into his pocket. "I always forget to check the eyes."

Bill looked at him apologetically, expecting the alien to be cross, but Whistler just looked miserable. Phly tinkled over to take his grey hand, but he barely seemed to notice.

"So," he said glumly, "You're just a boy, then."

Bill nodded.

"A boy?" said Tallulah. "I've met one of them before."

"Really?" said Bill, who had rather assumed he was the first to have fallen down a manhole several hundred miles deep.

"Yeah. Tall, nice teeth. Name began with a G."

"Ooh, yes," said Phly, smiling fondly. "I remember him. Grammar… Grimmer…"

"Graham?" suggested Bill.

"Oh, you know him, then?" said Tallulah.

"Er… no," said Bill. "Lucky guess. So, where is he?"

At this, the room fell quiet. Tallulah shuffled her feet, kicking up dust with her clumpy boots. Whistler looked even more miserable. Phly bowed her head, a faint hum of what sounded like a prayer escaping under her breath. Even the antelope looked sad, and it was asleep.

"Well?" said Bill, feeling nervous.

"He went…" began Tallulah, sounding unusually hesitant.

"They took him…" murmured Phly.

"He's gone…" said Whistler, grimly.

All three looked at one another with bleak faces, looked at the rusted iron door in the shadows, then gazed at Bill.

"*Down*," they whispered, all three together.

Bill stared. "Down?" he said. "But there isn't any more down. I fell forever. This is the bottom of the hole."

Whistler drew a deep breath, wiped a grey hand over his damp, bald head, and sighed.

"Bill," he said, heavily, "I think there are one or two things you ought to know."

Chapter Three

The Onion

... in which much is explained

Bill liked stories. He read them slowly, sinking deep into every page so as not to miss anything. He liked adventure stories best, tales of bravery and danger, and he had often found himself staring at the back of the wardrobe, or the cupboard under the stairs, and wondering, *"if... if... if... if only."*

And now here he was, living a story properly, and discovering that it was about as much fun as sitting in the dentist's chair waiting for the drill.

Tallulah had sat cross-legged in front of him. Phly had curled up by his side, resting her fuzzy head in the crook of his elbow. Whistler had stayed standing, his arms folded. Between them, they had made his head spin worse than a washing machine on a merry-go-round.

The first explanation had gone like this:

"The universe," said Tallulah, "is an egg."

"The universe," said Phly, "is the inside of a tree trunk, with one ring for every year."

"The universe," said Whistler, "is a well-fed Gracklebinder."

This was where the first explanation stopped, since Bill didn't know what a Gracklebinder was. On further examination, neither did Tallulah or Phly, but Tallulah shushed the alien before he had the chance to explain his explanation.

(For those who are interested, a Gracklebinder is a round beach ball of a fish, which floats around with its mouth open waiting for other, smaller Gracklebinders to accidentally swim into it. As a result, any large Gracklebinder will, when cut open, contain another, smaller Gracklebinder, which will itself contain another, smaller Gracklebinder, which will contain another, smaller Gracklebinder, and so on until whoever is cutting it up gets bored and chops up something less predictable.)

The second explanation went like this:

"The universe," said Tallulah, "is an eyeball."

"The universe," said Phly, "is a rosebud, waiting to unfurl its petals."

"The universe," said Whistler, "is a wheel within a wheel, like the Trimorphic Polarity Drive."

This was where the second explanation stopped, for reasons which probably don't need explaining.

Fortunately, the third explanation was more successful.

"The universe," said Tallulah, "is an onion. A great big onion, with lots of layers all on top of one another, and as you peel them off, the onion gets smaller and smaller, until you get right down to the sprouty bit in the middle."

"And that's where we are now, in the middle?" said Bill slowly, wondering if that bump on his head had done permanent damage.

"Ooh, no," said Phly, eyes widening. "It's a very big onion. Your journey was just a tiny little footstep."

"So we're *inside* the onion, somewhere between the outside and the middle?"

Phly nodded, earrings jingling.

"You got that much quicker than Graham," said Tallulah, then lowered her voice. "I think he was a bit dim, to be honest."

"How do I get back to the outside?" said Bill, peering up at the dark mouth of the hole above them.

Whistler sighed. "Always the same," he muttered. "Hundreds of worlds, and everyone thinks theirs is the most important."

"Um," said Bill, not wanting to be rude but feeling fairly sure of himself, "if the universe's an onion, then I do live on the outside. I mean, I've seen it, on TV. People have been into space and taken pictures."

"Space, eh?" said Whistler. "The vast starry blackness far above your skies? What makes you think that your 'space' is not another layer above yours? And that beyond its boundaries lie yet more, stranger layers of life?"

"I... I've never really thought about it like that," stuttered Bill, suddenly feeling even shorter than usual.

"Whistler's an explorer," said Phly, smiling fondly up at the alien. "He's making a map of the universe, of all the layers. He's ever so clever."

Whistler gave the elph a courteous nod. "Very

good, Phly. I am the Lord High Expeditioner of the Quxynggrotly, honoured with the task of continuing our many centuries of research. Ask me anything, anything at all."

"OK," said Bill, thinking. "How many layers are there?"

"Ah, a common question," said Whistler, "but a good one. The mapped layers number well over 300, though no one knows how many remain uncharted."

"Told you it was a big onion," said Tallulah.

"I myself have recorded data from 72," Whistler went on, puffing out his narrow chest. "I hope that one day I might have the privilege to be the first to record 100, but, of course, travelling between the layers is no easy task."

"It's not?" said Bill, thinking that falling down the manhole hadn't been particularly tricky.

"Oh, no," said the alien. "You see, the layers don't keep still. Your world, for example, is constantly spinning. Lovely place, by the way – excellent pizza, very good for the skin."

He rubbed his moist grey hands together, admiring them. Bill blinked, and wondered quite what the staff at the pizza restaurant had made of him.

"The other layers are no different," Whistler continued. "All rotating and revolving around one another. The hole between your world and the next is always there, just beneath the surface. Every now and then it joins up with a hole on the surface of your world and, if you happen to fall down the hole on the surface at just that moment – well, down you go."

"And then the hole moves again?" said Bill.

"Well, obviously," said Whistler. "If it stayed in the same place, someone might notice that people kept disappearing down a hole and never coming back, and they'd have the good sense to cover it up with a big rock. Of course, the layers all travel at different speeds. Some holes stay open for years at a time – you probably fell straight through several different worlds on your way here."

Whistler smiled brightly, waiting for the next question, but Bill had stopped listening. He stared up at the alien, and swallowed hard.

"Disappearing down the hole and never coming back?" he said, in a small voice. "You mean, I can't ever go home?"

The silence that followed wasn't what Bill wanted to hear. No one seemed to want to look at him.

"What," he said nervously, "happened to Graham?"

"The same as what happens to everyone who gets captured," said Tallulah, casting a bleak look at the rusted iron door. "They leave you in here, till you think they've forgotten all about you, and then... and then they take you to *Him*."

The elph and the alien nodded miserably. Tallulah took a deep breath.

"The Great Spondozo," she whispered.

Bill frowned. "Sounds like a magician," he said.

"Some say he is," Phly murmured, her melodic voice sounding muted. "A black sorcerer, who can climb inside your brain and tell you what to think."

"He has a vast army of Gatherers," said Whistler, grimly. "Guards trained to protect their evil master with their lives. Not to mention legions of spies. As for the man himself, no one knows where he came from; no one even knows what he looks like. But there's no question about what he wants: he's taking over the universe, layer by layer."

"He's, like, a *really* bad guy," said Tallulah.

"And what does he do with prisoners when they get taken to him?" said Bill slowly, not sure he wanted to hear the answer.

"Makes them his slaves," said Tallulah. "Steals their souls, fries their brains. You know, general bad guy sort of stuff."

"There are plenty of rumours," said Whistler, holding up a calming hand. "But to be honest, Bill, no one really knows."

Phly gave a tiny sniff.

"Because no one ever comes back," she sang, softly.

Bill gazed at the three dismal faces, and the dank, dripping room, and the cavernous hole up above, and thought about all that time spent staring at the back of the wardrobe, and wished wholeheartedly that someone, somewhere, had warned him he was going to find himself in the middle of a story in time for him to make himself a bit less rubbish at everything.

Tallulah stood up, rubbed her hands together, and attempted a cheery smile. "Never mind, eh?" she said. "Who's for a game of Scrabble?"

~★~

Three games of Scrabble later, Bill was beginning to think that having your brain fried might not be so bad after all.

Tallulah cheated wildly, throwing down words that couldn't possibly exist in any layer of the world, like 'Ttbki', and 'Mng'. Whistler argued with everything, whether it was made up or not, and constantly pulled the silver Knowletron out of his dungarees pocket to prove he was right. Phly played her own version, Zen Scrabble, which involved throwing the tiles into the air and seeing what words they wanted to make, while Bill struggled with letters that, no matter how many times he threw them back into the bag, would only spell out things like 'gloom' and 'doom'. There was shouting, tears, and more than a little pulling of hair, and no one was especially upset when the antelope put a stop to it all by waking up, walking across the almost-full board, and daintily eating a P.

"Hello, 'lope!" sang Phly, hopping up to give it a hug. "Did you have a nice sleep?"

The antelope blinked, then licked her face.

"Oh, good!" she trilled.

Tallulah rolled her eyes. "Phly, we've been over this, the antelope can't…"

"What's it doing?" said Bill, warily getting to his feet.

The antelope was standing in the middle of the Scrabble board, looking straight up at the dark hole above, twitching its long ears and sniffing. As they watched, it suddenly stiffened, then made a strange 'eef'ing sound, leapt a foot in the air, and bounded away to hide in a dim corner.

Seconds later, a large sack dropped from the hole above and landed on top of the paper tower. Hundreds of yellowed scraps fluttered into the air and rained down on them, like unusually boring confetti. Just as the scraps had settled, the paper tower wobbled, and shifted, and the sack tumbled off the top and landed smack bang in the middle of the board, sending letters skittering across the room.

Bill jumped backwards with a yelp, and landed on something bony that whistled when he hit it.

"See, I told you it could talk," sang Phly, beaming at the antelope as it attacked the string tying up the sack with its small, sharp teeth.

Rolling off the alien, Bill opened his mouth to apologize, but he was silenced by an unmistakeably familiar smell drifting towards him. It smelt like lazy Sunday mornings, and chilly Saturday teatimes, and waiting outside the cake shop while his mum pretended not to be buying doughnuts.

Bread. Warm, new bread, fresh from the oven.

Tallulah crawled over to the sack, emptying it out onto the floor. "Like I said, stuff falls down the hole all the time."

"And prisoners are no use if you let them starve to death," said Whistler.

"Maybe this time it'll be something nice," hummed Phly, with a hopeful look.

Bill stared at the three packages that now sat on the Scrabble board, as Tallulah swiftly unwrapped them. The paper they were wrapped in was plain and greasy, but his stomach was making excited noises at the smell alone.

The princess sat back on her heels and grunted. "Oh, pilf. That nasty slimy ham stuff, the yellow thing, and another one of those funny rocks, same as always."

Whistler pulled the nearest package towards him: a yellow slab, glistening slightly. With a shudder, he scooped up a yellow blob with his finger, and shoved it into his mouth.

"Urgh!" said Bill, unable to stop himself. "That's... you can't eat it like that!"

"It's not too horrid if you hold your nose," said Phly, stroking Bill's shoulder sympathetically.

"But... but..." said Bill, as Tallulah forced a fingerful down with a grimace. "But that's *butter*! And this is bacon! And this is bread!"

The three looked at him blankly.

"But that's everything you need to make bacon sandwiches!" he said, holding up the bread so he could smell it properly. As he did, he nudged the mouth of the sack, and a small red bottle rolled out.

"Oh, yuk, it's that horrible wine," said Tallulah, screwing up her nose.

"No!" said Bill, seizing the bottle happily. "This isn't for drinking, it's for putting on your bacon sandwiches. This is really nice food!"

The three faces stayed blank.

"Do we have anything to cook with?" said Bill, looking over at the pile of junk in the corner, and realising that the mouldy smell was probably coming from a large pile of discarded loaves of bread.

Phly giggled, then rubbed her hands together, blew on them, and held up her open palms. A flame danced there, flickering in her hands and somehow not burning her fuzzy skin.

"Wow," said Bill. "How did you do that?"

She shrugged shyly, obviously pleased.

"There's a scientific explanation," Whistler said loudly, clearing his throat. "A forest dweller such as an elph will absorb flammable saps and resins from the trees... which can then be lit by... er... chemical combustion with... er... well, it's very complicated..."

"Oh, shut it, Whistle-boy, and help me find some firewood," said Tallulah, crashing around in the junkpile, and hurling the occasional chunk of wood over her shoulder towards Phly. "How's this, Bill?"

She held up a couple of plates, a knife, and a dusty, blackened frying pan.

"Perfect," said Bill.

Half an hour later, they were sitting in a circle round a blazing fire, and the mouldy, slimy, wet doggy smell of their dungeon seemed to have been banished forever, to be replaced by the wonderful salty sweetness of fried bacon. It would have taken less time, but Tallulah and Whistler had an argument about who was going to be in charge of the cooking, Phly insisted on personally apologizing to each individual twig, stick and broken chair leg before adding it to the fire in case it was an old friend, and the antelope helpfully collected torn paper to start the fire off, which would have made very effective kindling if it hadn't been in an antelope's mouth. Bill, despite being the resident bacon sandwich expert, stayed several feet from the crackling fire, making sure that his scarf was tucked well out of the way.

(Bill, Bill's scarf, and naked flames were a dangerous combination. The tail of his scarf had once wandered into the campfire on a caravanning holiday, and smouldered away like the fuse on a stick of dynamite until he accidentally dipped it into a mug of cocoa, and put it out with a fizzle. He spent every Bonfire Night with his feet in a bucket of water, surrounded by piles of sand, after the single twig he'd poked into the town communal bonfire had caused the whole thing to topple backwards into a hedge, sending the flames speeding along the hedgerows like toppling dominoes, and reducing three fields of crops to black stubble. And he was almost certainly the only ten-year-old not to have candles on his birthday cake, after he had blown a little too hard at the ones on his ninth birthday, and ignited his mum's new net curtains.)

Bill busied himself with bread-buttering duties, and even found himself demonstrating how to slap the end of the tomato ketchup bottle to get lots out, although at home this was not considered a useful skill. True, some slopped onto the plate, and got on his fingers, but no one seemed to mind. In fact, they were all so busy wolfing down the sandwiches that there wasn't really room to talk, although Tallulah tried her best.

"This," she said, in a muffled voice as she shoved another wodge of warm bread into her mouth, "is the nicest thing anyone has ever eaten ever."

Whistler was making odd groaning noises accompanied by faint whistles, which to Bill sounded like he was in terrible pain, but from the rate at which the long fingers were snatching up sandwiches presumably meant the opposite. Phly was somehow singing while she ate. The antelope, which had politely turned up its nose at the elph's offer of a sandwich, tiptoed through their circle, delicately lapping up leftover drips of tomato ketchup.

They munched their way through the entire loaf of bread and all the bacon, and then curled up together in a warm heap at the bottom of the paper tower. Phly crawled onto Bill's lap, wrapping his scarf around her like a skinny blanket, and tucking her head under his chin. The fire popped and crackled as it burned, accompanying the gentle snoring of the antelope, who had fallen asleep on Tallulah's feet. Bill sat back, licked his fingers, and thought to himself that even if Tallulah had taken some persuading that there was a difference between 'cooked' and 'burnt to an inedible cinder', and even if they were prisoners, when you put all of it together, it would be hard to feel anything but contented.

"So, you three," he said with a yawn, "all just fell down a hole, like me?"

Phly nodded vigorously under his chin.

Whistler shifted awkwardly, dislodging a small shower of paper scraps. "Well, I wouldn't say *fell*, exactly…" he coughed.

"I didn't," said Tallulah, sighing. "Got arrested by a Gatherer patrol."

"For trying to stop the Great Spondozo?" said Bill.

"Stop the Great Spondozo?" said Whistler, sitting up in horror.

"Ooh, that's a good idea!" chirruped the elph, tugging at the leg of his dungarees. "Can we, Whistler, can we?"

Bill's eyes widened. "Oh no… I didn't mean…" he stuttered.

"I've heard stories of people trying to fight back; rumours of some kind of organized resistance," said Whistler seriously, gazing at Bill with a grave look on his face. "But the Great Spondozo has spies everywhere. What you're proposing would be highly dangerous."

"Proposing?" said Bill, alarmed.

"Come on, slimy, why not?" cut in the princess. "What are we going to do, just sit here and wait for him to come and suck our brains out? Or go and blow stuff up?"

"Boom!" squeaked Phly excitedly, jumping up and down on Bill's stomach and squashing all the air out of him.

Whistler sighed. "I suppose I'm not getting a great deal of exploring done in here," he said, eyeing a coughing Bill. "Tell me, what sort of a Plan did you have in mind?"

"Plan?" said Bill, feeling panicky. "I never said anything about a Plan!"

Whistler frowned at Bill. "What? You mean you don't want to stop the Great Spondozo, the most wicked being that has ever lived?"

"You don't want to smash his head in?" said Tallulah, smacking her fist into her palm for emphasis.

"You don't want to free all the slaves?" sang Phly, in a doubtful tone.

"Well… yes, of course," mumbled Bill, thinking that he'd never read a book where the hero said no to that sort of question. "But… well, I don't really know how."

"Pah! Details," said Tallulah, giving him an encouraging punch on the shoulder and rolling over.

"You sleep on it, Bill," mumbled Whistler, through

a yawn. "You'll come up with something in no time, I'm sure."

Bill opened his mouth to explain that he wasn't actually all that good at Planning, but Phly's eyes were falling closed.

"Tell us a story, Whistler," she murmured, sounding half asleep already.

The alien yawned again, then began to tell a long story about exploring, which involved many dangerous creatures and a lot of Whistler being very brave. Full of bacon sandwiches and with an elph lying on him like a hot water bottle with a heartbeat, Bill felt his eyelids drooping, and dropped off into a sound sleep.

When he opened his eyes again, the fire had died down to its embers, leaving the cell dark and chilly. There was an eerie silence, broken only by dripping from some damp corner. Bill shrugged, wondering what could have woken him, and was just settling back into the fluffy mound of paper when he heard it.

A creak.

He stared in horror at the rusty iron door, waiting for it to open, but then a sudden movement in the shadows caught his eye. He whipped his head round, peering into the gloom. There was another creak, then a low growling sound.

Something was in the junkpile.

Chapter Four

The Trapdoor

… in which antelopes are helpful

Bill froze, and stared breathlessly at the shadowy mountain of junk in the corner. By the faint, yellow light of the bulbs he could make out a black shape, moving close to the ground, and scrabbling about at the edge of the pile. It stopped for moment, wrestling with something buried there, then it seemed to sense him watching, and stood up.

It was hideous. Atop a skinny body swayed a huge, misshapen head, with a row of thick ridges on the crest. To Bill's horror, it staggered backwards towards him, stumbling as if blind. Then, with a muffled 'eef', its head fell off.

Bill stifled a yelp of fright, and glared at the antelope. It blinked at the wellington boot which had been stuck on its head, then trotted back to the junkpile and began nosing through it, tugging at stray bits of string and cloth and metal.

Very gently, Bill unwound his scarf from the sleeping elph, and climbed out of the pile of sleepy bodies.

"Careful!" he whispered, hurrying to catch a falling teacup as the antelope took hold of an umbrella handle with its teeth and hauled it out of the pile. "You'll wake the others up!"

The antelope blinked at him, with a look that seemed to say waking them up wasn't something it was too bothered about, and carried on burrowing through the junk.

Bill put the cup carefully on the floor, and looked properly at the junkpile for the first time. There really was a phenomenal amount of rubbish stacked there. Pieces of broken drainpipe, shoes with the heels falling off, empty marmalade jars. Bent spoons, and strings of old washing lines, knotted around coat hangers and old hairbrushes. There were big things, too, so big you wondered how they had fitted down the hole, like a fridge with no door, and an aquarium with a crack in it. And there was a load of stuff which Bill couldn't imagine why people had thrown away, like a pile of sleeping bags, and a neat coil of rope, and a camping stove, and a book about how to use the stove, and a book about climbing, and a book about how to build really tall ladders.

Bill stared at the pile, then looked up at the hole.

"I think someone's trying to help us," he murmured.

The antelope blinked at him, then thrust its nose further into the junkpile, butting a bundle of ski poles out of the way. Moments later it emerged, a coil of washing line looped around its small horns and a square blue package, about the size of a pizza box, in its teeth. The antelope stepped backwards, tugging at the package, waggling its head to free it. The washing line, which was knotted deep into the tangle of junk, resisted the pull. The antelope tugged again; the washing line creaked and strained. With one last mighty heave, the antelope dug in its hooves and finally wrenched the blue square free, and as it turned to Bill to drop it at his feet, the tangled washing line brought the entire pile of junk crashing to the floor.

The sound would have been enormous anywhere, but in the dungeon, it sounded like someone had dropped sixteen orchestras onto a pile of balloons during a thunderstorm.

"Don't shoot, don't shoot!" shouted Whistler, sitting bolt upright in a panic and whistling sharply.

"Oi! Antelope!" shouted Tallulah, rubbing her eyes crossly. "If I wanted an alarm call, a lick on the face would've done fine!"

Phly skipped over to Bill's side and took his hand. "Look, look, Bill's rearranging our pile of gifts!"

"Um… sorry," said Bill, shuffling his feet and looking around at the scattered junk, which now took up half the floor. He glanced at the antelope, which was standing where the junkpile used to be, and doing some sort of tap-dance in an attempt to unloop the washing line from its head.

"What's that?" said Tallulah, yawning as she picked up the blue package. "Self-inflating life-raft," she read.

"For use in emergencies only," said Whistler, peering over her shoulder.

"I wonder what this bit does?" hummed Phly, pulling a blue string dangling from the package.

A hissing sound filled the room, and the life-raft began

to move, and grow, slowly unfolding itself as it filled with air.

"Nice one, Phly," said Tallulah, rolling her eyes.

The raft pushed the bits of drainpipe and old shoes out of the way as it grew fatter and rounder, touching one wall, nudging the bottom of the tower of paper, brushing against their feet, until it was as big as a king-size bed.

"Ooh, a great big blue thing!" sang Phly, leaping into the raft and hugging its squashy inflated sides.

"S'pose it might make somewhere comfy to sleep," said Tallulah, kicking it and sending Phly bouncing into the air with a tinkly giggle. "Thought everything in that pile was just rubbish. How did you find it, Bill?"

"The antelope," said Bill, pointing.

They all stared at the antelope, which had disentangled itself from the washing line, but was still dancing, now slightly breathlessly.

Tallulah wrinkled up her nose. "I always thought that 'lope was a bit funny in the head," she said.

"No!" said Bill, exasperated, and pointing more firmly. "*Look*!"

The antelope was tap-dancing on top of a large, square, wooden trapdoor, set into the stone floor.

"A door! Hello, door!" piped Phly, scurrying over to stroke the brass handle.

"A secret entrance," sniffed Whistler. "I always knew there had to be one."

"Didn't manage to find it, though, did you?" The princess smiled at Bill. "Well done, matey."

Bill opened his mouth to say he didn't think he'd had much to do with it, but the antelope blinked at him, then hopped into the life-raft and curled up into a ball, as if it didn't want to be disturbed right now. The elph, meanwhile, had tugged on the brass handle and opened the door up, so she could properly greet the other side of it. A chill wind blew up from below, setting the fringes of her cloak jingling, and swirling dust and torn paper around the room.

Tallulah peered over the edge of the hole. "It's very dark," she said.

Bill was trying to keep back from the edge, but his foot nudged a fallen milk bottle, which rolled slowly towards the hole, and toppled over.

"Excellent plan," said Whistler, nodding. "Testing the depth. Quiet, everyone."

They waited.

And waited.

And waited.

Tallulah sat down, swinging her legs dangerously over the hole's edge.

Still nothing.

Then, just as Bill was about to step backwards and trip over a cricket bat, they heard it. Quiet, echoey, and very far away, but unmistakeable.

Splosh.

"Ooh, what a lovely noise, can we drop more things?" sang Phly.

"*No*," said Tallulah firmly, hauling the elph back to safety by her cloak.

"I knew it wouldn't work," said Whistler, shaking his head. "Terrible plan, Bill, what were you thinking?"

"Um," said Bill, looking at the antelope curled up in

the life-raft. "Actually, I think it might work."

Phly looked at the raft, then clapped her hands together. "Yes!" she trilled. "We can throw the antelope down the hole, and it can drink whatever water is at the bottom so we won't drown!"

The antelope 'eef'ed quietly from the bottom of the raft.

"Actually," said Bill, "I thought maybe we could drop the life-raft. With us in it."

"No, no, no," said Whistler testily. "That wouldn't… we couldn't possibly…"

"Top plan, let's do it," said Tallulah, slapping Bill on the back.

Taking care not to puncture it, the princess and Bill dragged the life-raft over to the trapdoor, and put it over the top. It was much too large to fall straight down, but when the antelope stood up in it, the middle of the raft sank downwards. Very carefully, Bill stepped in: the centre of the raft sank deeper, its inflated sides lifting off the floor. Tallulah grabbed Phly, who had wandered off and was trying on broken shoes, none of which would stay on her tiny feet. The pair of them climbed in, and there was a squeaking, scraping sound as the bottom of the raft began to squeeze through the hole.

"I think perhaps we should - make some calculations - anticipate variables -" stammered Whistler, hesitating at the raft's side.

"Yeah, right," said Tallulah, grabbing him by the dungarees and hauling him into the raft on top of everyone.

With a tearing noise, the life-raft folded itself in half

like an inflatable blue omelette, and plummeted down the hole. Bill was squashed under someone's thin, pointy elbows; then he was kneeling on someone's tousled, tangled head; then there was something warm and furry pressed against his cheek, which he hoped was a mossy cloak and not a bit of antelope. Ringing in his ears was the shrill, high-pitched wail of someone whistling, loudly, in terror.

He lost his breath. He lost his sense of up and down and left and right. He lost quite a lot of hair to someone's clutching fist. And just as he was about to lose his breakfast, there was the most enormous splooshing sound, and the raft stopped falling.

Bill opened his eyes, to discover that he was face down in the raft, with his nose tucked behind Whistler's knee, and his legs somewhere above him. Rolling over, he turned himself upright, and pulled his hair out of his eyes.

The raft had landed on an underground river running through an enormous cavern. The craggy walls towering over them on either side shimmered, silver and purple veins of glowing fluorescent quartz twining through the rock. The quartzes ran on below the water, making its surface sparkle and glimmer and sending pale silvery lights flickering across the vast arching roof. The raft bobbed calmly on the waters, gliding past the shining rocks.

"We did it," wheezed Whistler, sounding stunned. "We escaped."

"Woohoo! Teach Spondozo to try and lock us up," yelled Tallulah triumphantly, laughing as she listened to her words echo back to them.

Bill was too relieved to say anything, and he just leaned back and rested his head on the raft's side, gazing up at the dancing play of watery light on the roof of the cavern with his mouth open.

"What's that noise?" said Tallulah.

Bill listened. Somewhere under the rushing echo of the water and the chiming of the elph's cloak there was a definite hissing sound.

"Oh, look, a big hole in our boat!" sang Phly excitedly, pointing at a large tear in the blue plastic. "I wonder what's inside?"

She tugged at the edges of the hole, pulling them wider to see in, then squeaked and fell backwards as the air rushing out hit her in the eye. Bill felt the soft cushion of the raft under his head give slightly, as the hissing sound got louder.

"Phly!" shouted Tallulah crossly, jumping over and trying unsuccessfully to seal up the hole by sitting on it.

"Now, crew, everyone stay calm," said the alien, letting slip a faint whistle.

Bill swallowed as the raft began to pick up speed. The water was getting choppier, and forming crested waves that lifted them in the air then dropped them suddenly, tipping them sideways in a shower of spray. He gripped the side of the raft, feeling the wet blue plastic give worryingly under his fingers, and wished fervently that his swimming abilities extended beyond those of a very dead donkey. He looked at the antelope, hoping it might somehow have a secret pocket with a puncture repair kit in it, but the antelope was standing up in the middle of the boat, its ears lying flat against its head. Bill followed its gaze, and gulped.

The cavern was opening up into a huge rock chamber. As the surging river carried them closer, the rushing sound of water was building to a roar. At the centre of the chamber was a vast whirlpool, spinning and churning and spitting great sprays of foamy water into the air.

"Oh, pilf," said Tallulah, in an unusually quavery voice. "Whistler, what do we do?"

The alien shook his head helplessly, staring at the swirling water with wide yellow eyes.

"Let me see!" sang Phly, almost tumbling overboard as a huge wave crashed over the edge of the deflating raft, soaking them all.

The sinking raft spun round in the water as the current took hold. For one second they seemed to stop dead, hanging on the edge of the whirlpool. Then they plunged downwards, the crashing water sucking them under.

"Hang on!" yelled Tallulah.

Bill shut his eyes and held his breath and clutched onto the side of the raft as the water closed over them, wet and cold and black, and spinning him around and around and around, until his chest felt like bursting and his hands had lost their grip, and then it was slowing, and getting lighter, and not so wet, and really rather breezy.

Bill risked opening one eye, and then the other, and realized that he was falling. Again. And just as he was thinking that it was really about time that he stopped falling, and that he was really quite fed up of it now, he hit the ground, with not so much a whump as a damp squelch.

The raft (if you could still call it a raft, since all the air had gone out of it and it now looked more like a wet tablecloth) had landed in the middle of a small copse of trees, at the top of a hill. Above them, clouds drifted in a grey-blue sky, letting the occasional shaft of sunlight through. A light wind ruffled the grass, making Bill shiver.

Beside him someone sneezed, a high, melodic sound, accompanied by jingling. Scraping wet curls out of his eyes, Bill saw Phly close by, soggy and crumpled and looking very much like a damp flannel. Nearby, Whistler was glumly wringing out the legs of his dungarees. Tallulah was tipping water out of one large black boot and looking unusually clean, while the antelope was shaking itself, and spraying them all with cold droplets of water.

"Well, that was exciting!" sang Phly, watching the antelope and then shaking herself too, with a wild jingling sound. "Where are we, Whistler?"

The alien took the silver Knowletron from his pocket, flipped it open, emptied some water out of it, then tapped it into life. The globe of light flickered uncertainly, then cleared.

"Just one moment, crew," said Whistler, coughing officiously, "and I'll have everything under control." He walked to the edge of the trees, holding out the Knowletron as if scanning for something.

"Aha! Habitation!" he said, his finger skimming through the glowing images. "Let's see… castellations… primitive stonework…"

Intrigued, the others followed him. Stretching out before them was a landscape littered with castles, turrets and towers, as if someone had scooped up all of Britain, thrown away the ugly bits, and dropped the rest in the nearest valley. There were mottes with wooden baileys and square towers of rough-hewn stone, huddled beside huge castles with pointed roofs, cloistered courtyards and flying buttresses. Pennants and flags fluttered in the wind, among twists of wood smoke; in the distance was the faint boom of cannon fire, and the shouts and whinnies of battle.

"Hmm… yes…" muttered Whistler, his finger still stabbing at the globe. "Very familiar…"

"Familiar?" said Tallulah, miserably. "I should say it's familiar. This, my friends," she said, sitting down and sighing heavily, "is my home."

Chapter Five

The Three Kings' Heads

… in which Tallulah goes home,
and Bill goes to the pub

Bill stared at Tallulah, who was tearing up fistfuls of grass and ripping them into small angry pieces.

"This?" he said, looking in awe at the countless castles nestled in the valley below. "This is your home?"

As the princess nodded, Phly let out a tinkly gasp of delight, then flung her soggy arms around Tallulah's neck. "You must be so happy!" she sang.

Tallulah shook her off crossly. "Of course I'm not happy," she muttered, then noticed the looks of disbelief on everyone's faces. "Well, OK, it's better than being stuck in a stinky old dungeon," she said grudgingly, "but honestly. Of all the layers in all the universe, why did we have to fall into mine?"

"But… but this place is amazing," said Bill. "I mean, you live in a castle. I've always wanted to live in a castle."

He ignored Tallulah's contemptuous snort, and was just picturing himself asleep in a four-poster bed so big even he couldn't fall out of it, surrounded by rich tapestries and flickering torches, when the antelope trotted over and butted him in the knee. With a yelp, Bill tumbled backwards, and landed in the nearest bush.

"What did you do that for?" he yelled, clutching his knee, before realising with alarm that the bush he'd landed in seemed to be moving. All around them the leaves had begun to quiver; there was a sound like far-off drums, and the ground seemed to throb beneath his feet.

"Most peculiar," said Whistler, holding up the Knowletron and walking to the edge of the copse. "I'll just…"

"Get down!" yelled Tallulah, leaping forward and rugby tackling him to the ground. Seconds later, louder than thunder and close enough to spatter the alien with mud, a small army galloped past.

Six black horses, teeth bared, lips frothing at their bits, muscular flanks glistening with foam. Astride each horse, a warrior, upright in the stirrups, clad head to toe in coal-black armour. Hoarse voices shouting; a horn sounding; hooves tearing up the turf.

And then they were gone, galloping away down the slope towards the fortresses in the valley below.

"Blimey," breathed Bill, clambering out of the bush and crawling cautiously forwards. At the edge of the copse, a churned path of black mud cut like a scar across the grassy slope.

"Ooh, what lovely beasts!" sang Phly, cantering around on her hands and knees and neighing.

"Clearly an attack force," said Whistler, frowning at his

muddy dungarees. "Team, I suggest we remain here until the battle's over. Primitive warfare can get messy."

As if in agreement, a ball of fire flew over the hills on the far side of the valley, exploding at the foot of a wooden fort in the castle city and setting its foundations alight.

"That might take a while," said Tallulah, visibly cheering up as another fireball whistled over the hills, and crashed through the thatched roof of a long barn. "They started fighting a few years ago, and I don't think anyone's planning to surrender any time soon."

"What are they fighting about?" said Bill. Black smoke began to pour from the barn, followed by several singed-looking people, and he started to think that perhaps living in a castle wasn't quite so glamorous after all. But before Tallulah could answer the ground began to thrum again, and above the distant booms and crashes of battle came the unmistakeable pounding of another army.

Six white horses, nostrils flaring, necks plunging forward, straining at the reins. Astride each horse, a warrior, clad head to toe in shining bronze armour. The leaves trembled; great chunks of turf were ripped up and hurled into the air; sunlight flashed off burnished metal.

But this time the thrumming didn't stop. Seconds later came another army, of six dun horses, with six riders in rust-red armour, and then six greys with six silver warriors, and six palominos with six riders in emerald. On and on the armies came, till the sixes mingled and the sunlight sent many-coloured flashes glinting off the polished armour. The Knowletron bounced out of Whistler's pocket and skittered along the grass. Phly curled up into a ball, pulling her cloak over her head as its fringes tinkled wildly. Even the antelope looked a little unnerved.

"What's happening?" Bill mouthed to Tallulah, shrinking back as another flurry of hooves passed dangerously close to their hiding place.

Tallulah waited until the torrent of passing horses began to slow to a trickle, then tapped her ear. "Listen!" she said, scrambling to her feet and moving to the edge of the bushes.

Bill strained his ears, and as the din of hoof beats died away, he could make out the sound of a bell ringing.

"A call to arms of some kind?" said Whistler, tucking the Knowletron back into his pocket, and irritably trying to rub grass stains off his knees.

"Call to the stomach, more like," said Tallulah, as Bill joined her. She pointed down the hill to a tall clock tower at the centre of the castle city, with a pointed roof like a witch's hat. "It's lunchtime."

"There's a war on, and everyone stops for lunch?" said Bill.

"Hey, everyone needs lunch," shrugged Tallulah, "and a good thing too. If we're going to stop Spondozo, we'll have to hire an army, and by lunchtime they're usually a bit bored with trying to kill each other."

Phly uncovered her head. "New friends, hooray!" she sang.

"Jolly good," said Whistler. "You know the territory, Tallulah, you lead the way."

"Whoa!" said Tallulah, holding up her hand. "Those people down there have never seen an alien, or an elph, and an antelope isn't exactly going to blend in. We're escaped prisoners: we've got to be inconspicuous." She gave Bill a quick look up and down. "Well, as inconspicuous as possible. Don't worry, we won't be long."

Whistler began spluttering a protest, but Tallulah was already walking away, gripping Bill's wrist in her hand and dragging him behind her. "Just keep out of sight," she called over her shoulder, as she squelched off through the mud. "And whatever you do, don't move from that copse."

"Wait!" yelled Bill, limping after her, and shivering as the breeze hit his damp clothes. "I don't think I should... I mean, maybe I should stay with the others?"

Behind them he could hear Phly enthusiastically arranging a game of hide-and-seek. Ahead of them, the castle city continued to destroy itself. The wooden fort that had caught fire was now listing at an odd angle as flames ate away at its foundations, but its occupants continued to fire a volley of arrows towards a square red-brick folly. Meanwhile, armoured figures swarmed up the walls of a half-ruined stone tower. Great plumes of black smoke rose into the sky from several different places, shadowing the sun.

"Thought you'd always *wanted* to live in a *castle*," said Tallulah, giving him a sly grin.

"I'm sorry," mumbled Bill, stumbling on the end of his scarf as she dragged him onwards. "I didn't expect it to be so... dangerous."

"Oh, the knights aren't so bad," said the princess blithely. "Sure, they've got big swords and crossbows and they spend all day throwing cannonballs at each other, but they don't mean any harm by it."

Bill ducked as another fireball sailed over their heads, feeling unconvinced, but as they drew closer to the city he noticed that although every castle seemed to be at war with every other castle, nobody seemed too bothered about actually hitting each other. In fact, Bill thought, it was almost as if they were trying not to. The six black knights who had first ridden past them certainly didn't seem particularly intent on destruction. Their horses were tethered near the twin towers of a castle on the outskirts of the city, and the knights were now resting at a trestle table outside the gates with their feet up. As he watched, a copper-haired woman dressed in a embroidered gown of burgundy silk and a very stained apron emerged from the castle, to a raucous cheer from the knights. She was carrying a wooden tray, with six pewter goblets containing something frothy, and a bowl of what looked like peanuts.

Tallulah groaned and made a face. "Queen Enid," she muttered.

Bill stared at the woman handing out drinks, and the knights dropping silver coins into her apron pocket, and the wooden square swinging on hinges from the crooked flagpole, with its painted picture of a fox being ridden by a tiny man in bright silk clothes.

"She's a queen," he said, clearing his throat uncomfortably, "and she works in a pub?"

"We've all got to make a living," shrugged Tallulah.

Bill frowned, and then looked at Tallulah's messy hair, tatty frock and clumpy boots, and reminded himself that if princesses could look like her, queens were probably free to do as they pleased. He was about to ask what Tallulah's mum did, since she was presumably a queen too, but the ground was flattening out, and their muddy track had met up with a cobbled road. They had arrived.

To Bill's surprise, in spite of the explosions, the smoky air, and the occasional pile of rubble, the city looked remarkably well cared for. Each castle stood in its own patch of ground, separated from the next by cobbled paths with neatly mown grassy banks. The road they were on ran right through the city, leading towards the tall clock tower with the pointed roof. Bill could see rows of litter bins, wooden tubs of flowers in doorways, and only a couple of black puddles where someone had spilt their boiling oil.

He began to ask who was in charge of keeping it all so tidy, when a loud voice brought them to a stop.

"Halt!" bellowed the voice.

With a jolt Bill turned round, and found himself standing nose to point with a rusty, but still quite sharp-looking, pike. Swallowing hard, he looked up. Attached to the pike was a portly man, squeezed into an ancient suit of armour. The helmet had lost its visor, the breastplate was dotted with holes like a pepper pot, and one arm and half a leg were missing completely, leaving him slightly tilted to one side.

"Who goes there?" boomed the man, staring importantly over Bill's head.

Bill gazed helplessly at the man, realising he was standing guard at the gates to a large manor house. It looked like the sort of place aunts insisted on taking him to on bank holidays, except that through the diamond-paned windows Bill could see rows of shelves stacked high with what looked like tins of food, and toilet rolls, and in the back yard was a train of rusty shopping trolleys.

At the guard's feet stood three painted signs. The first declared:

TRESPASSERS WILL BE MURDERED

The next, slightly smaller, read:

slowly

while the last, almost too small to read, said:

(with forks)

"Well?" said the guard, giving Bill's nose a little jab with the pike, and finally looking down at them. "Oh," he said, retracting the pike and grinning. "Sorry, Tallulah, didn't realize it was you."

"Yeah? Next time, look before you poke," said the princess, as Bill rubbed the sore spot on his nose. "Bill, this is Wolfgang. Used to work for my dad. Wolfie, meet Bill. Sir Bill, that is, a boy from… er… Boyland."

"Boyland?" said Wolfgang, eyeing Bill with suspicion. "Never heard of it."

"It's that way," said Tallulah, pointing randomly off into the distance. "Just over that hill. And left a bit."

Wolfgang shrugged, then pulled a crumpled notebook out from his breastplate. "Sir Bill… Boyland…" he muttered, laboriously writing it down, then turned to Tallulah. "Nice to have you back, 'lulah. And I won't be the only one who thinks so."

Tallulah coughed awkwardly, then hurried Bill away down the road. "Just a flying visit, Wolfie, no time to stop," she called over her shoulder.

Moments later they were brought to a halt again before a crumbling tower rather like an old chapel, if old chapels sold fishing equipment. Bill stood quietly, trying to ignore the notice that read:

NO ENTRY
on pain of dentistry

while Tallulah introduced him to the spotty youth guarding the entrance with a pitchfork.

"See you around, Tallulah," said the guard cheerily, as she tugged Bill urgently onwards. His name was taken down at a cottage in a walled bailey that apparently sold stationery, and again at the entrance to a shoe shop in a stone keep.

"Aren't we supposed to be being inconspicuous?" whispered Bill, anxiously stepping round a scorched crater in the middle of the path outside a turreted castle filled with pots and pans. "I mean, we are escaped prisoners."

"It'll be fine," said the princess, waving her hand dismissively. "By the time anyone notices we're here, we'll be long gone. Besides, you can't get into the city without getting on the list."

"Is it some sort of town register?" said Bill, coughing as they passed a still-smouldering pile of rubble.

"Nah, just a list of invasions."

"Invasions? But I'm just walking down the road,"

protested Bill.

"Didn't you see all the 'Keep Out' signs?" said Tallulah, as the road narrowed, taking them into the heart of the city. "You crossed their borders without permission. That's an invasion. Nothing to worry about, mind: it's Boyland they're at war with really, and that doesn't even exist."

Bill thought wistfully of the safe copse up the hill, suspecting that Tallulah and he had quite different ideas of what was worth worrying about. She dragged him on through another few streets, then pulled him to a halt and began sniffing the air.

"What are you doing?" Bill said, but as he opened his mouth, an odd taste flooded into it, and a peculiar smell swept up his nose. It was sweet and savoury, like salty honey, or creamy brown bread: unfamiliar, but strangely comforting, like wearing someone else's jumper.

"What *is* that?" said Bill, breathing in great lungfuls of the smell.

Tallulah grunted mysteriously, then shoved him off the main road into a dark, cramped lane between two castles, holding her finger to her lips. Seconds later, there was a loud bang, and a yellow flare flashed in the sky. At once all sounds of fighting stopped, and the air filled with the noises of cheering and running feet. The main road where they had been standing was suddenly filled with rushing people, some wearing armour, some dressed in elegant gowns and furred cloaks, and all hurrying in the same direction, laughing and slapping each other on the back as they ran. Bill turned to look down the lane, and saw another swarm of people racing past its other end, all looking equally excited.

After a few minutes the hordes of people slowed to just a handful of old men hobbling along and looking crossly at their slow legs. Then the deserted streets fell quiet.

"Where have they all gone?" said Bill. "And what's that amazing smell?"

"You like it, then?" said Tallulah dismally.

"Oh," said Bill, realising that wasn't what she'd wanted to hear. "It's just not anything I've smelt before, I suppose…"

As he spoke, the princess's face turned from gloom to alarm.

"I mean, it's nothing special," spluttered Bill hastily, but Tallulah slowly shook her head, staring dumbly over his shoulder. Behind him, Bill heard heavy footsteps approach, and he froze as a meaty hand reached over him to grab hold of her.

"Tallulah von Stuffelheim," a deep voice boomed, right above him. "Do you have any idea how long I've been looking for you?"

Bill craned his neck around. Towering above him was a huge man, dressed in scraggy ermine and red velvet, with piercing blue eyes, unruly dark hair, a long black moustache, and a smudge of dirt on his chin.

"Hi, Dad," said Tallulah, weakly. "How's it going?"

~★~

Half an hour later Bill was sitting in a pub called The Three Kings' Heads, and beginning to understand why Tallulah wasn't overjoyed to be back home.

Her father, whose name was King Fernando, had quickly forgotten his anger, and was now so overjoyed to have his daughter back that he could hardly bear to put her down. He bounded around her like an excitable puppy, dashing away to fetch warm scratchy blankets to dry them off with, then rushing back to give her another hug in case she vanished again. To Bill's surprise, Tallulah endured his fussing with barely a grumble, and only winced a little when he planted a sloppy kiss on her forehead.

But Fernando wasn't the problem. The family castle was made up of one vast room, with a spiral staircase leading up to a narrow tower at the back. Although it was the middle of the day, the glassless windows faced onto a dingy alley: the only light came from a few guttering candles and the dim glow from the fireplace, where a blackened pot of nasty-smelling stew bubbled away. The smell of stew mingled with mould and damp; the air felt clammy, and the piles of furniture stacked up around the walls were thick with dust and cobwebs. Bill didn't know anyone else who lived in a pub, but he'd never imagined that one could feel so cold and empty.

"It didn't used to be like this," whispered Tallulah to Bill gloomily, as she sent her father off to make tea. "A few years ago, this was the busiest pub in the whole city. Most nights they'd be queuing out of the door. Then all the fighting started, and *she* arrived, with her oh-so-fabulous Cheese Beer, and that was that."

"Cheese Beer?" said Bill distractedly, looking around and trying to imagine the room minus the grime and shadows.

"Queen Enid's Olde Worlde Homee Madee Secret Recipe Cheese Beer, only available at The Fox and Jockey," said the princess, wrinkling up her nose. "They send up a flare when the next batch is ready, and everyone goes running."

"*That's* what the smell was," said Bill, feeling a hungry tingle in his stomach at the memory. Realising he was smiling, he quickly breathed in a big noseful of the stew, which made him feel sick and made Tallulah look much happier. "I'm not very fond of cheese," he lied.

"Well, you're the only one," she said, squashing a passing spider with the heel of her boot. "We haven't had one customer since she got here. Dad's tried all sorts of special offers to coax them back – buy one drink and get thirty-two free, that sort of thing – but no one wants to know. Mum got fed up and ran off with Duke Eric the milkman, and after that I think he sort of lost it. Personally I'd rather go over there and smack stinky old Enid's head in, but Dad won't have it. Keeps saying he'll find something up his sleeve one of these days."

At this, King Fernando reappeared bearing three mugs of tea, and sat down heavily next to his daughter.

"Nice and strong, just how you like it," Fernando said, tousling Tallulah's hair fondly before turning his bright blue eyes on Bill. "Now then, Sir Bill, we must get properly acquainted. My daughter here tells me you're the finest sword in all Boyland."

Bill tried to cover his surprise with a swig of tea,

which was very stewed and tasted strongly of dust.

"If you don't mind me saying so, Sir Bill, you look a little short for a soldier," the king said doubtfully.

"They start them young over there," Tallulah said airily, giving Bill a wink. "In fact, Sir Bill rescued me from a dragon when I was lost in the woods. Slashed it to bits, he did. I would've been toast if he hadn't come along."

"Can't tell you how grateful I am, Sir Bill," said Fernando, clasping Bill's hand in his vast paws and shaking it energetically. "I'm afraid my daughter has a tendency to get herself into trouble when left to her own devices."

Bill smiled wanly, and concentrated hard on looking knightly.

"I'm particularly glad you brought Tallulah back today, Sir Bill," Fernando went on, standing up and puffing out his capacious chest, "because today is a very special day. You may have noticed that business here at The Three Kings' Heads is a little slow…"

"He's smelt the Cheese Beer, Dad," said Tallulah.

"Oh dear," said Fernando, discouraged. "But!" he said, waggling a finger at them triumphantly, "after today, no one will be drinking Cheese Beer! Not once they've tasted my latest concoction!"

Fernando hurried over to the fireplace, and began crashing about with pans and ladles. His enthusiasm didn't seem to have passed on to Tallulah, though, who squirmed with embarrassment.

"This happens a lot," she whispered, watching him apologetically.

Bill leaned forward. "What was all that about dragons?" he whispered.

She stood up. "I'm just going to show Bill the rest of the castle, Dad, all right?"

"Whatever you like, my dear," Fernando called, his head buried in a cupboard.

The two of them climbed the spiral staircase, passing a few tiny rounded rooms before arriving at the top of the tower, where the flat roof made a sort of balcony. It was very chilly, and Bill kept a careful eye out for more spiders, but the view was fantastic: he could see above many of the spires and towers, and even beyond some of the hills, to other clumps of castles nestling in green fields. And it was easy to find The Fox and Jockey, from the crowds of people gathered outside it, the sounds of laughter and cheering, and the potent salt-sweet smell of the Cheese Beer pouring from the chimney.

"Listen, don't go all squeaky about it," said Tallulah, turning her back firmly on the merriment. "But I could hardly tell him I'd been captured by the Great Spondozo, could I? He'd be so relieved I escaped he'd never let me out of his sight again."

"How *did* you get captured?" asked Bill.

"I went looking for Queen Enid's hidden vault, the one where she keeps the secret recipe. Made it past the first few locks, but I must've tripped an alarm somewhere. Next thing I know there's a pilfing great Gatherer squad right there waiting to pick me up - and no prizes for guessing where they took me."

Bill nodded, trying not to blush. Falling down a hole whilst running away from the school bully didn't seem quite such a good reason to end up a prisoner as a daring break-in to help your father. Not that his parents would want him to start stealing things for their benefit; and even if they needed some other kind of help with the paperclip factory or the butcher's shop, he was sure they wouldn't ask him. He was pretty sure they wouldn't forget he'd gone missing quite as quickly as Fernando had, either. They weren't the hugging kind of parents at the best of times, but a lost Bill was the sort of thing that made them particularly annoyed, and it was beginning to look like it might take him a while to get home. Always assuming he *could* get home.

"The Gatherers," said Bill, in a small voice. "What are they like?"

Tallulah puffed out her cheeks, grimaced, and was about to say something, before she seemed to think better of it. "You don't want to go worrying about them," she said, not quite meeting his eye. "Not before you have to."

Bill shivered, though the wind was no colder than before, and he nestled his chin deeper into the warm folds of his scarf.

"Nah, our army'll deal with them," said Tallulah, brightening up at the prospect. "Trust me, my dad's a terrible gossip. Once he's spread it around I've got a fearsome dragon-slaying warrior with me, they'll be jumping at the chance to fight the Great Spondozo. Especially if we leave them time to have a bit more Cheese Beer."

"About that… the fighting the Great Spondozo thing…" Bill began, anxiously.

"How's the Plan coming on?" she asked. "I think our main problem might be spies. And finding Spondozo. And not getting killed. But I'm sure you'll work something out."

"I don't think…" Bill began again, but tapping footsteps announced the arrival of a pink-faced Fernando, carrying a tray of three rusty goblets as tenderly as a sleeping baby. In each was a thick, lumpy brown mixture.

"Lamb Beer!" said the king reverently, handing them round. "I've got another batch brewing downstairs, but this is one I prepared yesterday. I've been chilling it on the windowsill specially."

Bill looked at the skin which had formed on the brown lumpy surface, and wondered whether the smell or the taste would be the first to make him throw up. But Fernando was looking at him expectantly, with the slightest hint of panic at the edge of his excitement, and he looked so terribly hopeful that Bill knew he would just have to close his eyes and drink. Slowly, he raised the goblet to his lips.

"I say, whatever is going on down there?" exclaimed Fernando, startling Bill into dropping his cup and splattering brown glop all over everyone's shoes.

Bill turned to look where Fernando was pointing. Standing amongst all the many-coloured knights outside the Fox and Jockey he could just make out what looked like a wizard, or maybe a monk. He was wearing a long blue cloak, which was shiny, as if it was made of some sort of plastic, and had a huge hood completely covering his face. Slung over his shoulder was a sort of green sparkly backpack, and at his feet was a very odd-looking dog wearing a blue hat.

"Haven't seen him round here before," said Fernando. "Perhaps a friend of yours from Boyland, eh, Sir Bill?"

As they watched, the cloaked wizard swayed slightly, and began waving his arms around. The knights around him were laughing and shouting, raising their glasses and knocking them together. Then, in an instant, the mood changed. The laughter turned to jeering, then to snarling. Glasses were set down, swords were drawn, and suddenly the wizard was surrounded by sharp silver points flashing in the sunlight.

Tallulah cleared her throat, then turned to her father with a strained smile.

"I'll be right back," she said, then thrust her goblet into Bill's hand, shoved past him, and disappeared down the stone staircase.

Chapter Six

The Grand Re-Opening

... in which there is a party

Bill watched in horror, as Whistler (for it was
undoubtedly him under the blue plastic cloak) continued
to sway and wave his arms. The green backpack on his
back was wriggling, and the antelope had bared its
teeth, although the effect was slightly diminished by the
blue plastic hat. All around them surged an angry crowd
of knights.

King Fernando, meanwhile, was staring at the top of
the staircase down which his daughter had just fled.

"Perhaps she felt it needed more salt," he said. "What
do you say, Sir Bill?"

"I'm sorry I dropped it," said Bill, meaning it, as the
Lamb Beer he'd spilt was seeping through his shoes.

"No matter," said Fernando sympathetically. "Have
Tallulah's, I'm sure she won't mind."

Bill nodded unhappily, and noticed that he could
now see the princess sprinting through the quiet streets
towards The Fox and Jockey.

"Well?" said Fernando, face flushed with anticipation.

"Do you like it?"

Bill stared at the scummy surface of the Lamb Beer. The distant shouting was growing louder and angrier; Fernando was beginning to frown and peer over the battlements to see what all the commotion was about. There was only one thing for it. Bill lifted the goblet, and poured every last drop of Lamb Beer down his throat.

Lumpy gravy and old cabbage slithered down in one revolting swallow.

"Delicious," Bill rasped, the cabbagey whiff of his own breath making his eyes water. "Let's go downstairs and get some more."

Bill gripped Fernando's sleeve, as much to keep himself upright as to hurry the king away, and lurched towards the spiral staircase. The slimy soles of his shoes hit the puddle of spilt beer, and his feet disappeared from under him, sending him tumbling down the stone stairs, closely followed by Fernando. He caught a glimpse of whirling ermine, and then his head hit something hard, and knocked him out.

The next thing he knew, he was lying somewhere cold, dark and oddly shaped. There was a strange-tasting fur on his tongue, and a terrible throbbing in his head just above his left ear. Unwillingly, he prised open his eyes, and realized he was lying in what must have been Tallulah's bedroom. The sky outside the narrow slit of a window had grown dusky, but by the flickering of a candle he could make out tatty clothes strewn carelessly across the floor. In place of posters, the walls were decorated with rusty swords. The bed had been built into the curved walls of the tower, making it impossible to lie straight, and his feet were dangling off the side in confusion.

Bill closed his eyes and tucked his feet under the scratchy blankets, but now he was awake he could hear a low murmur of conversation. He could also definitely hear a tinkling, jingling sound. Then, much louder, he heard a low groaning, as if someone was in great pain. Wrapping the blanket around him, and taking the candle from the windowsill, Bill stepped over the scattered clothes, and crept down the spiral staircase.

The huge room was in murky darkness, broken only by the occasional candle and the glow of the fire. The antelope, still wearing its blue hat, was snoring on the hearth, and Phly was playing hide-and-seek with a spider, but Tallulah and her father seemed to have had some sort of argument. Fernando was slumped in a chair by the fireplace, cradling a pot of Lamb Beer and letting slow tears roll to the ends of his moustache and plop into the brew, while Tallulah was sitting dejectedly at the kitchen table. Even more worrying was the sight of Whistler sitting bolt upright beside her, the hood of his blue cloak pulled down over his face. His whole body was trembling, and Bill could hear a mournful whistle that seemed to be accompanied by the faint whiff of cheese.

Bill hovered at the bottom of the stairs, wondering if he might be better off back in bed, but Phly's spider scuttled over to his feet, and the elph bounded after it.

"Bill!" she sang, wrapping her arms around his legs. "Bill's not dead, Bill's not dead!"

"Dead?" said Bill, wincing as his headache complained, and keeping an eye out for the spider. He suddenly found himself engulfed in musty ermine robes.

"Sir Bill!" cried Fernando, squeezing him tightly, then standing back to gaze at him, before sweeping him into another overwhelming hug. "So wonderful to have you back!"

"Thanks," mumbled Bill breathlessly.

"Sleep well, did we?" said Tallulah, giving him a half-smile.

Bill nodded, rubbing his sore head and looking up at the king. "I really am sorry," he said. "I didn't mean to worry anyone."

Fernando dropped on one knee, and clutched the trailing end of Bill's scarf nervously. "Now, Sir Bill, if there are apologies to be made, it's me that should be making them," he said in a throaty voice. "Tallulah has reminded me that sometimes I get a little carried away in the kitchen. That sometimes my recipes might not be… quite up to standard. After all you've done for my daughter, Sir Bill, to think that I could've poisoned you…" He paused to wipe his nose on his furry sleeve.

"But you didn't," said Bill. "I just fell down the stairs."

The king blinked through his tears. "Fell?" he said.

Bill nodded.

"You mean, you really did want some more? My Lamb Beer really is *delicious*?"

Bill opened his mouth, but a little hopeful light had come on in the king's damp blue eyes, and he nodded instead. Fernando's moustache ends crinkled upwards in a crooked grin not unlike his daughter's, and he rose eagerly to his feet. Bill took a step back, fearing another hug, but Fernando turned to Tallulah.

"You see?" he said, his face pink with delight. "My Lamb Beer was just the beginning! As soon as your druid friend finishes meditating, there's no telling what wonderful concoctions he and I could create! This party's going to be *fantastic*!"

Giving Bill a last grateful squeeze, he dashed over to the fireplace, and began rattling pots and pans. The antelope woke up, blinked at the king, then disappeared into one of the kitchen cupboards, nosing the door firmly shut behind it.

"Party?" said Bill. "Druid?"

Tallulah shushed him with a look, and in a low voice filled him in. It seemed that Whistler, Phly and the antelope had waited in the copse until Whistler had decided that an explorer really ought to be out exploring – a decision which had hit him, by an uncanny coincidence, at the precise moment that the smell of Cheese Beer had drifted up from the city – and, in order to maintain their disguises, Whistler had joined the crowds at The Fox and Jockey and ordered a pint.

"I only had one mouthful," moaned the alien, his voice sounding oddly muffled. "For purely scientific purposes, of course."

"Apparently that was all it took," said Tallulah, checking her father was busy over the fire, then lifting Whistler's hood up with a grimace.

Bill gasped. Whistler's tiny, wrinkled walnut of a head had swollen up like a balloon, and the usually moist skin was now dry as paper. There was a greenish tint to his eyes, which now looked small and lost in the vast expanse of his face.

"Quxynggrotlys have very sensitive constitutions," Whistler whimpered. "Must be some kind of allergic reaction. We explorers often face such dangers in our travels." He gazed plaintively at Bill. "Does it look very bad?"

"No, no, you look fine," Bill lied, leaning back as another cheesy breath wafted in his direction.

"I think you look lovely," sang Phly, holding Whistler's quivering hand and tinkling as her robes quivered with it.

"Well, the customers at The Fox and Jockey didn't. By the time I got there, they were about ready to chop his head off," said Tallulah. "They don't take too kindly to people insulting Queen Enid's beer."

"They said all sorts of things about King Fernando's beer, though," chipped in Phly, brightly. "They said it was like drinking earwax. And they said that it was a good thing the goblets were always so dirty, because then you couldn't taste the…"

Tallulah clamped a hand over the elph's mouth and ignored her muffled squeaking.

"I could hardly let them get away with that, could I?" she said, casting a rueful look at her father bustling round the fire. "So I told them we were having a grand re-opening party, with everything for free. I made out that Whistler was this big mysterious druid, who could brew up amazing potions – "

"Potions that make people turn small and green and tinkly!" sang Phly, escaping from the princess's grasp and hopping on one foot.

"Well, I had to explain you away somehow," said Tallulah. "Anyway, I made them a promise. If we can't offer them something as good as Cheese Beer, then that's it. The von Stuffelheims will admit defeat, and The Three Kings' Heads will close its doors forever."

Bill's eyes opened wide. "What did your dad say?" he whispered.

"Well, at that point he was a bit more worried about having poisoned you," said Tallulah, "but now? You can see for yourself."

Bill watched as Fernando skipped around the kitchen, tossing a handful of black peppercorns into the pot, and humming a chirpy tune as he stirred.

"He thinks this is going to be the best day of his life."

~★~

An hour later, The Three Kings' Heads was almost unrecognisable.

The floor had been swept, and the stone flags polished until they were almost shiny. The cobwebs dangling from the ceiling had been replaced by Bill's stripy scarf, which hung like woolly bunting in loops from rafter to rafter. Benches and tables had been pulled in from a shed outside, and laid with a collection of goblets, mugs, flowerpots, and eggcups; dozens of candles lined the walls in clusters, giving the chamber a warm orange glow. It didn't look exactly sophisticated, but it did at least look like a pub.

While Bill and Tallulah had scrubbed and swept, the others had set about making an enormous mess in the kitchen. Fernando and Phly had ransacked the kitchen cupboards for new ingredients (except for the cupboard with the antelope in it, which snarled when anyone opened the door as if to suggest that antelope was not on the menu), and the table before Whistler was piled high with the entire contents of the von Stuffelheim larder.

Unfortunately, the spread was less than inspirational. With a groan and a shaky wave of the hand, Whistler had dismissed Phly's enthusiastic proposals of Earwig Beer, Mouse Poo Beer, and beer made from Unidentifiable Contents of Jar, and once these had been excluded, there wasn't much to choose from. Fernando started a few experimental pots bubbling over the fire, but his insistence on squirting in a dash of his moustache-stiffening cream ("Adds a subtle hint of lemon," he claimed) made each new brew unappealingly lumpy. By the time a hot and dusty Bill and Tallulah came to help, even the king was looking discouraged.

"What we need," said Whistler weakly, "is to go back to first principles. This Cheese Beer that the knights are so keen on, what's in it?"

"It's a secret recipe, you flinker," said Tallulah.

"Not the precise recipe, just the basic ingredients. This 'cheese', for example. How would we make that?"

"It's made from milk," said Bill, guessing from the creamy smell of Queen Enid's beer that cheese here was not too different from cheese at home.

"Milk?" said Whistler, suspiciously.

"White stuff," said Tallulah. "Comes out of cows.

If you leave it to go off for a bit, it goes hard, and then it's cheese. There's a bit here somewhere," she added, unearthing a crumbly chunk of what looked rather like cheddar.

Whistler whimpered and clutched his stomach. "And 'beer'?" he said, in a faint voice.

"Not much call for the plain stuff round here," said Fernando, taking a dusty bottle down from a shelf and pouring brown frothy liquid into a glass. "But for a simple brew like this, you mash up certain plants with water, then leave it for a month or so to ferment."

"That means wait for it to go off, too," said Tallulah.

Whistler stifled another moan, then gingerly picked up the chunk of cheese and dropped it into the glass of beer.

Everyone stared. The surface of the cheese fizzed for a few seconds, then it sank to the bottom.

"It doesn't look much like the other Cheese Beer," sang Phly, in a doubtful tone.

"Maybe it's the wrong kind of cheese," suggested Bill.

"Or the wrong kind of beer," said Tallulah.

"Never mind, Sir Druid," said Fernando, laughing nervously. "You'll come up with something, we've still got plenty of time before the party's due to…"

He looked at the clock, and his cheery bright blue eyes faded. "Twenty minutes," he said, quietly.

There was an uncomfortable silence. From outside came a distant cheer, and the sound of far-off footsteps headed their way. Bill looked at Tallulah, hoping she might have one last idea, but she had gone to sit next to her father.

"Sorry, Dad," she said, giving the grubby ermine of his sleeve a little stroke. Fernando gave her a feeble smile, and ruffled her hair.

The distant footsteps drew closer.

The candles flickered and dimmed in the gloom.

And then, with a crash, the door to one of the kitchen cupboards flew open and out fell the antelope, looking rather bedraggled and clutching in its teeth a lumpy brown sack. It staggered forward and dropped the sack on the floor, letting it fall open. Three greasy, paper-wrapped parcels fell out.

For a moment, they all simply stared. Then Tallulah wrinkled up her nose, and grinned.

"You don't suppose those parcels might be..." she said.

The antelope tapped the sack with its hoof. A small red bottle rolled out across the stone floor.

Tallulah, Whistler and Phly stared at the bottle, then at one another, then, all at the same time, shouted, "Bacon sandwiches!"

"Clever Bill!" sang Phly, flinging her arms around his neck. Bill hugged her back, opening his mouth to point out that he hadn't had much to do with it, but she hopped away to help the antelope haul two more sacks from the cupboard. Bill stared, wondering how such a small place could have held three big sacks and an antelope. As the cupboard door swung open, he thought he glimpsed a cobbled street, and the fire flickered suddenly as if a draught had rushed through an open window. But then the antelope nudged the cupboard shut with its nose, and sat decisively in front of it.

Once bacon sandwiches had been explained to Fernando, with the parts about Tallulah being locked in the Great Spondozo's dungeon carefully removed, The Three Kings' Heads became a flurry of excited activity. Fernando got the fire blazing; Tallulah set to work with the frying pan; Whistler sliced the bread; Phly did the buttering; and Bill slapped the bottom of the ketchup bottle. By the time the crowd had gathered outside, the room was filled with the glorious smell of warm buttered bread, crisp bacon and tomato ketchup, and on each table sat a pile of hot bacon sandwiches.

Giving Tallulah one last rib-crushing hug for luck, Fernando unbolted the main doors, and flung them open.

"Welcome to The Three Ki-" he bellowed, before being thrust aside by a surging mass of armour. The knights poured through the doors, shoving, laughing, and shouting various rude remarks about milkmen as they filled the room. There were a few smirks and mocking looks when they saw the plates of food, but once the burly black knights had tucked in, the jeering gave way to hushed murmurs of awe, swiftly followed by shouts of "More!" The rust-red knights snatched a plateful from the green knights' table, and gobbled them down so fast the green knights couldn't be sure who'd stolen it. The orange knights demanded extra ketchup; the purple knights preferred them without butter. Every seat was taken, every table surrounded by an eager army jostling for second helpings.

The plates kept on spinning around the room, passed out piled with sandwiches, returning moments later without a crumb left. But the frying pan never emptied, the ketchup bottle never ran dry, for every time supplies seemed to be running low, the antelope would emerge breathless from the cupboard with another brown sack, and everyone was far too busy frying or slicing or buttering to stop and wonder where it was all coming from.

Eventually, after every knight in the room must have eaten at least four rounds of sandwiches, and one of the black knights was rolling on the floor in full-stomached delight, the constant demands for more died down, and the frantic sandwich-making slowed to a halt. Bill looked around the crowded room, crammed with cheerful faces smeared with ketchup, and suddenly felt an arm sweep him up onto one of the tables. He looked down, and saw Fernando's bright blue eyes twinkling up at him. The king clapped his hands together, and, slowly, the noisy room fell quiet.

"Everyone, I give you the finest swordsman in all Boyland, the slayer of dragons, and the inventor of the bacon sandwich – Sir Bill!"

There was a huge cheer. Everyone was staring at him, smiling and applauding. Over by the fireplace, Whistler, Phly, and especially Tallulah were beaming at him proudly. Bill blushed scarlet, feeling slightly scared, extremely embarrassed, and more than a little bit pleased.

Within moments he was surrounded by a huddle of excited knights, all wanting to shake his hand and slap him on the back and hear tales of his fabulous dragon–slaying exploits.

"How tall was it?"

"Did you get singed?"

"I've heard they get grumpy if you poke them in the eye. Is it true?"

By the time one of the knights had shyly asked Bill to autograph his helmet, the embarrassment was becoming too much.

"Really, it wasn't anything special," Bill mumbled. "It was a very small dragon. Not very fiery. I think it might have had a cold. And a limp."

The knights went on nodding and staring at him in admiration.

"I mean," Bill stumbled on, "I'm sure you've all killed far more dragons than I have."

At this, the knights stopped nodding, and started to clear their throats and look at the floor. One, wearing unmenacing lilac armour, coughed uncomfortably. "We don't really do much of the proper fighting these days," he said.

"Couldn't, even if we wanted to," said another, in green, holding up a dull, blunt sword.

"But," said Bill, looking round and seeing that all their weapons were rusted and broken, "but I thought you were all at war with each other. All the time."

"Ah," said a rust-red knight, looking shifty. "See, it's not really what you'd call a *conventional* war."

"It's not?" said Bill.

"Nah," said the rust-red knight. "See, in a conventional war, you all keep fighting until one side wins. That's how we used to do it. There was a new invasion practically every day of the week. Good times, they were. I mean, every now and then you might get cut down by a hail of arrows, or have your skull cleaved in twain by a mighty axe. But we had a laugh."

The rust-red knight sighed fondly at the memories. Bill nodded politely.

"Well, it couldn't last, could it?" he went on. "We'd just seen off another invasion from the emperor of the islands just off the coast, and we were all looking forward to having a bit of a rest till we invaded him next week, when *they* turned up."

The rust-red knight paused, glanced around the room warily, then leaned in close. "The *Gatherers*," he said, in a low whisper. "Didn't stand a chance against that lot – and neither did anyone else. Once the Great Spondozo was in charge round here there was no point anyone invading anybody else, and then we didn't have anyone to be at war with any more. And you know what that'd mean."

"Peace?" suggested Bill.

"Unemployment," said the lilac knight, shaking his head sadly. "We'd have lost our jobs right away. So there was only one thing for it: we'd have to get the kings and duchesses and lords and whatnot round here to declare war on each other. That way, they couldn't ever sack us, and we could have a little agreement between ourselves that we wouldn't really try to hurt each other."

"Oh," said Bill, failing to keep a note of disappointment from his voice.

"I know, it's not very honourable," said the green knight with a sigh. "But even being a bit of a fake knight's better than nothing."

At this, Tallulah poked her head into the admiring circle around Bill, and gave him a wink. "I think I might have a way around that little problem, matey. How would you like to go back to the good old days, eh? All that stabbing and hacking and chopping people up?"

She grinned encouragingly. Bill thought that she wasn't making it sound all that appealing, but the knights looked intrigued.

"You mean... proper violence?" said the rust-red knight.

"Actual stabbing?" said the lilac knight.

"And a full package of benefits, including horseshoe insurance and at least fourteen days paid holiday?" said the green knight.

"Sure," said Tallulah, confidently waving her hand. "We're going on a quest. You remember them: a chance to travel, meet new people, fight some of them..."

"And what are you questing for, Sir Bill?" said the rust-red knight, in awed tones.

"The... er..." said Bill, frantically searching for something vaguely questable. "The Holy... Snail."

"Oooh," chorused the knights. They muttered for a moment amongst themselves, then the rust-red knight rose to his feet, and drew his sword.

"Sir Bill, I swear on this sword you shall have our allegiance!" he said, emphatically stabbing it into the table before them. With a crack the rusty blade snapped, leaving the knight holding a small jagged stump. He gave Bill an embarrassed smile, and they retreated, the lilac knight giving him a sympathetic pat on the back.

Bill stared at the broken blade poking out from the

table, and gave Tallulah a worried look. "That's the army we're going to defeat the Great Spondozo with?" he whispered.

"Oh, it'll be fine," she whispered back. "They were quite good at being at war a few years ago, they'll get the hang of it again. Which will give you plenty of time to polish up that Plan."

Bill opened his mouth to protest, but with a giggle she was gone, off to rescue Phly who had tried on one of the silver knights' helmets, and was stumbling about bumping into things. Fernando was in the middle of the crowd, bellowing with laughter, and looking even happier than he had when Tallulah had first come home. Whistler was looking almost like himself again, and was talking intently to a knight in a quiet corner, secretly tapping away at the Knowletron. Even the antelope seemed to be enjoying itself licking up stray drips of tomato ketchup from the floor.

Bill weaved his way towards the front door and stepped out into the street. It was now quite late, and the air was chilly after being in the warmth of the pub, but it was quieter, and he felt like being away from the crowds for a while.

There was a tap on his shoulder.

He sighed, turning around and gazing up at a very tall knight in grey armour, who he didn't recall seeing in The Three Kings' Heads.

"Are you the famous Sir Bill of Boyland?" said the grey knight, in a not particularly friendly voice.

"Er... yes," said Bill, starting to wish that he wasn't.

The grey knight stared at him, then nodded to

someone behind Bill. There was a sudden rustling noise, and Bill caught a glimpse of a second grey knight before an enormous sack was thrown over his head. Strong arms tied his hands together, lifted him off the ground and hurled him across the back of a horse. With a jingle of leathers and a clatter of hooves, he was whisked away into the darkness.

Chapter Seven

The Bank

... in which a rescue is launched

Bill had never ridden a galloping horse before. As he bounced along, he had to admit that he wasn't exactly riding one now. With his hands tied behind him and a sack over his head, what he was currently doing was not falling off a horse, and even that was only because of a heavy hand pressing on his back. By the time the thundering hooves began to slow down, Bill was feeling so sore and sick and dizzy he would have been relieved, if it wasn't for his lurking suspicion that at the end of the journey, things were not going to get much better.

The grey knight steadied the horse and hefted Bill to the ground without a word, prodding him forward. Bill stumbled blindly through a doorway, feeling the air around him grow warmer. He turned corners, wound up and down spiral staircases, stooped through narrow passageways, with the grey knight always behind him, prodding him forward, catching him if he tripped, but never saying a word. The party back at The Three Kings' Heads was probably still going on, he thought miserably.

No one would have noticed he was missing, and even if they had, they wouldn't know where he'd been taken. He didn't, and he was there.

Finally, they arrived in an echoey room, filled with quiet voices. Feeling a finger poke him in the spine, Bill stepped forward, and the room fell totally silent. He had the sinister feeling that he was being watched by hundreds of people.

"And who do we have here?" said a loud voice.

"Sir Bill of Boyland, my lord," answered the grey knight behind him.

"Oh, good," said the voice, sounding unpleasantly treacly. "Do carry on, everyone, don't mind us."

Slowly the hushed voices built up again to a steady hum.

The feeling of being watched didn't go away.

"Well, take the bag off him, then," said the voice, sounding rather impatient, and making Bill jump. A moment later, the sackcloth was pulled away, and Bill found himself staring into the grey eyes of a disarmingly smiley man. He was dressed in a grey pinstriped suit, over which he wore a short purple cape trimmed with white fur. On his neat silver hair sat a delicate golden circlet, studded with tiny white gems; his smooth-skinned hands sparkled with rings. He looked very much like the people Bill's father invited around for important dinner parties, except none of them had ever kidnapped him.

The man in the grey suit looked Bill up and down, still smiling. "You're a little shorter than I expected," he said.

Bill tried not to blush, and stared round the vast

chamber as the grey knight untied his hands. The ceiling must have been 50 metres high; three rows of tall, diamond-paned windows spanned the walls, one above the other. Between the windows hung flaming torches, but by their flickery light he could see that the floor was covered in spotless pale blue carpet, and he was fairly sure he could make out the faint hum of air conditioning.

They were standing in a long aisle running the length of the room, flanked on either side by row upon row of wooden desks, all facing towards the middle. At the desks sat hundreds of dark-haired, pale-faced men and women, all wearing matching pinstriped suits, with purple fur at the collar and cuffs. In front of each of them was a large pile of papers, and they were scribbling away, murmuring to each other, and occasionally casting a glance in Bill's direction.

"Not even asking what I want from you, eh?" said the man in the suit, nodding with admiration. "Yes, I can see why they think you're dangerous."

Bill swallowed uncomfortably, as the man turned and began to walk up the carpeted aisle, beckoning him to follow. Bill hurried after him, trying not to notice the mutters and whispers that ran along the rows of people watching them.

"Is this because of the bacon sandwiches?" Bill said, wondering if this man was some relation of Queen Enid's.

The man shook his head, as they reached a huge desk at the end of the aisle with an imposing black leather chair behind it. On the wall above hung a series of portraits of him in various smiling poses, strolling through a park with a Dalmatian snapping at his heels, and shaking hands with someone important-looking in a uniform. Below the portraits hung a purple velvet curtain, with silver tasselled string draped across it as if to seal it shut. The man settled into the leather chair, and gestured at a smaller chair in front of the desk.

"Is it because of the *quest?*" said Bill anxiously, sitting down.

"In a manner of speaking," said the man smoothly.

Bill suddenly felt queasy with fear, and took a deep breath. "Are you... the Great Spondozo?" he whispered.

"Good gracious, no," said the man, laughing. "Terribly flattering of you to think so, but I'm afraid not. My name is Owen Silva. Not that the big boss downstairs and I aren't well acquainted, of course," he added, tapping the side of his nose with a well-manicured finger.

"You mean, you work for the Great Spondozo?" said Bill.

"I take care of business for him, yes. Being an evil genius intent on taking over the universe is dreadfully hard work, you see," Silva said, sighing theatrically. "Quashing rebellions, making sure everyone's adequately scared of you, the endless paperwork. There simply isn't time to take care of everything yourself."

"I've never really thought about it," Bill confessed.

"So of course you'll understand why someone like you causes us a bit of a headache," Silva went on, smiling again.

Bill frowned, and shook his head.

"Oh, you must have seen the way things work around here. All those hopeless knights, throwing rocks at each other all day, rebuilding their castles all night, and then getting up in the morning and doing it all over again. All that effort just to keep their jobs, when all the while every penny they earn comes directly to me. A convenient arrangement for us, of course. An evil genius is an expensive one, right, Sir Bill?"

Silva gave him a conspiratorial wink.

"And the knights seem contented enough – with a little help from a certain secret recipe," he went on. "We get the occasional ripple of unrest, an attempted robbery every now and then, but generally we can leave them to get on with it. An ideal arrangement for all concerned. But, sadly, one easily disrupted. Just imagine what would happen if a young, brave knight arrived and reminded them what real battle was like?"

"What would happen?" asked Bill warily.

"They'd make a rather sizeable army, that's what would happen," said Silva. "And if they stopped attacking each other, and attacked the Great Spondozo instead…"

"What would happen then?" asked Bill, feeling a bit more hopeful.

"Oh, well, they'd all die horribly," said Silva, depressingly quickly. "The Great Spondozo's Gatherers are the finest fighters in the universe, with the biggest, ugliest weapons imaginable. Anyone even thinking of attacking them would have to be insane. But all it takes is for one bright young thing to remind those knights of the glory of battle…"

Bill coughed uncomfortably, fearing that the situation was getting out of control. "I'm not actually a brave and famous knight, you know," he said. "I'm just a boy who fell down a hole."

Silva looked down at Bill, amused. "Sorry, Sir Bill, I'm afraid you can't fool me with this disguise of yours. Wandering around like you're just some undersized, clumsy schoolboy with a silly haircut. We know better, eh?" He tapped the side of his nose again, and gave Bill a knowing smirk.

Bill looked cheerlessly at the floor. "So what are you going to do with me?" he asked, rather nervous about the answer.

"Not entirely sure," said Silva, leaning back and flipping his feet up onto the desk, revealing perfectly polished grey shoes. "I've sent a messenger down to the centre of the universe to see what the boss wants to do with you. He's always on the lookout for talented spies. Don't suppose you'd be interested in working for the most evil genius the universe has ever known?"

Bill stared, and thought that it was the sort of question proper heroes were asked in films, and proper heroes always leapt up and shouted things like, "You'll have to kill me first!" But there were a lot of people quietly working, and disturbing them seemed rude, so he simply shook his head.

"Ah, well," said Silva. "Looks like you'll be for the chop, then. Very nice to meet you, though." He leaned forward and shook Bill's hand. "Now, if you could just go over to the back of the room, where you came in, my friend will take you to the workshop until the execution order comes through." He flashed Bill a smile, then busied himself with some papers.

"Execution?" said Bill, alarmed. "But I don't need to

be executed. I haven't done anything."

Silva shook his head. "Yes, I hear that a lot. Off you go then. *Next!*"

Bill turned in the chair, to see a large sack with feet walking up the carpeted aisle, prodded along by a grey knight. The knight jerked his head at Bill, motioning him out of the chair so the next prisoner could sit down. Bill walked slowly back down the long carpeted aisle, trying to ignore the constant whispering and muttering of the identical workers. At the far end he was greeted by another faceless grey knight, and was ushered silently down a long, winding stone staircase.

Twenty minutes later, Bill was sitting at his own wooden desk, feeling dismal. The room he was in was almost identical to the one upstairs, all pale blue carpet, flickering torches and rows of bent heads, scribbling away. But here the walls were lined with grey knights, and behind each row of desks ran a heavy chain, padlocked to shackles on the ankle of each worker. Bill had tried to protest as the metal cuff snapped closed around his leg, but the grey knight merely grunted, and dropped a stack of papers onto the desk, along with a rubber stamp with an X on it, and a red ink pad.

"Stamp each page, then pass it to your left," said the knight gruffly, and stomped away.

Bill picked up the first sheet. Written across the top was 'Receipt', followed by a bizarre shopping list:

1 (one) wagon, wood
1 (one) flagon, pewter
1 (one) dragon, dead, pref. stuffed

Underneath was printed 'Despatched', and a date, and beneath that 'Received'. There was a large space with a dotted line, and the words 'stamp here' written in tiny letters.

"*Psssssssst!*"

Bill jumped, and looked to his left. There was an old woman at the next desk, dressed in a faded version of the grey uniform, the purple fur at the cuffs and collar looking matted and worn. Her gnarled hands were covered in green ink, and she was clutching a rubber stamp like his.

"Hurry up!" the woman whispered again, nodding at the sheet in his hand and glancing furtively round at the guards.

Bill nodded apologetically, and pressed the stamp first into the ink, then onto the paper, leaving a shiny red X on the dotted line. Then he passed it to the woman, whispering, "Sorry." She shook her head crossly, stamped a large green X next to Bill's, and deftly flicked the page over to the desk on her left.

Bill frowned, as the next man added another X to the line, and passed it on. Leaning forward, he watched as the page made its way down the row, each person stamping an X on it and passing it on, until it was far down the line and out of sight. Bill looked at the rows of workers in front, and behind, and saw that they were doing the same, some with rubber stamps, some with pens, some with hole punches.

"*Psssssssssssssssst!*" said the old woman again, looking more annoyed.

Bill glanced at the next sheet, which also had 'Receipt'

written at the top, and was for the despatch of:

1 (one) longbow, yew
1 (one) long bough, oak
1 (one) horse trough, chestnut

Bill stamped it, and passed it over.

"You're not supposed to read them," said the woman, snatching it from him and holding her hand out for the next.

"Why not?" whispered Bill, stamping a receipt for '3 (three) leather jerkins, sizes small, medium and large'. "What are they for?"

"Bank business," said the woman, darkly.

"Bank business?" said Bill. "But this isn't a bank, it's a dungeon. I'm just working here while…"

The old woman nodded impatiently. "While you're waiting to be executed, yes," she muttered, leaning over and lifting Bill's hand up and down to stamp a few more sheets.

Bill gazed at the rows of people; what Silva had said upstairs was starting to make more sense. "You mean everyone here is waiting to be executed?"

"Of course," she hissed, grabbing Bill's rubber stamp off him and thumping it frenziedly on his scattered pile of receipts. "Would you do a job where you stamp meaningless bits of paper all day if they hadn't chained you to the spot?"

The old woman's inky fingers snatched another few sheets off his desk, and Bill wondered just how long she'd been chained there, stamping away. Forlornly, he was reaching for the next receipt, when there was a loud creak from the far end of the room. At the end of the carpeted aisle, three grey knights were struggling to heave a massive oak door open.

The cool evening air blew in through a huge portcullis, decorated with twists and twirls of wrought iron. Bill was so busy watching the portcullis slowly rising up, he nearly failed to notice that waiting outside were Tallulah, Fernando, Whistler (still wearing his blue plastic cloak), and an enormous number of knights.

Bill felt a little leap in his stomach. He half expected the knights to charge in shouting and waving swords above their heads, but they came in quite slowly, chatting amongst themselves and admiring the carpet. Bill caught a glimpse of a tousled head, and stood up awkwardly to wave. The chain round his ankle yanked him back to his seat with a yelp, and he just had time to catch Tallulah's eye, before she knelt and fiddled with something too low down for him to see.

"*Pssssssst!*" hissed the woman again. "Stop staring at the customers and get on with it!"

Bill absently stamped a few sheets, and passed them on with a tiny smile.

"They're not customers," he whispered. "They're my friends, and they've come to rescue me."

There was a tinkly rustle at his feet, and a small, green, excited head appeared from under his desk.

"Have we?" sang Phly, opening her dark eyes wide with enthusiasm. "Oh good, I love rescuing things. What's the Plan?"

"I haven't got a Plan, I'm chained to the floor," said Bill, staring at the elph in confusion. "You mean you haven't come here to rescue me?"

Phly shook her head, jingling softly. "No. Lots of the knights decided to come on our quest with us, and we thought we should get all their money out of the bank so we can buy them some really shiny new weapons, and an extra horse for Whistler, because he likes horses. After that, we were going to come and look for you. But now we don't have to, because we've found you already! Have you thought of the Plan yet?" She rested her head on his knee, and looked at him expectantly.

Bill gazed helplessly at the scribbling rows of uniforms, and the line of grey guards along the back wall, and thought to himself that taking money out of this bank might be harder than anyone was expecting. In a shadowy corner, he spotted one knight set apart from the rest, with a purple sash across his chest, and a bunch of keys dangling from a hook in the wall behind him. At the knight's feet, he could just make out a small dark shape, with four legs, pointy horns, and very sharp teeth, which were at that moment reaching up to snatch the keys off their hook.

Bill looked at the elph. "I think maybe we should try to distract the guards," he said.

Phly nodded, and ducked out of sight before he could say anything else, which was lucky, as what he was going to say next was, "but I have no idea how." Bill peered round at the knight with the purple sash. The four-legged shadow was nowhere to be seen, and neither was the bunch of keys, but the rest of the grey guards were scanning the rows of workers keenly.

Bill jumped, as Phly popped up from under the table

again. "Tallulah says she thinks it's a very good Plan, and that you should start it straight away," she sang, quite loudly.

"Shh!" hissed Bill, looking up and seeing the grey knight with the purple sash weaving through the rows towards him. Gulping, he grabbed the elph's head and shoved it down under the desk.

"What's that under the table?" barked the knight.

"Nothing?" said Bill, hopefully.

"Hello!" sang Phly, popping her head up and giving the knight a jingly wave.

The grey knight glared at the two of them, and with a noise like fingers down a blackboard, slowly drew a very large sword. Bill stared at his own face reflected in its shiny surface, and noticed that he looked quite terrified. Then he clamped his eyes shut, thought nasty thoughts about the bacon slicer in his mum's butcher's shop, and waited for the blade to fall.

There was a loud crash from the doorway.

"Drop your weapons! This is a robbery!" bellowed a deep voice.

Bill sneaked one eye open. Standing in the doorway was a hefty black knight, whom Bill had last seen rolling on the floor of The Three Kings' Heads. There were streaks of tomato ketchup dribbled down the front of his armour, mingling with the froth of an awful lot of spilt Cheese Beer. He held one sword raised high over his head, and another rested, rather unsteadily, against the neck of a grey knight, who was kneeling on the ground with his hands on his head and a rather embarrassed look on his face.

"Oh, no, not again," muttered the green-fingered woman under her breath.

No one moved.

"I said," shouted the black knight, with a little belch, "this is a robbery!"

A vague murmuring rose from the clump of knights gathered in the middle of the room. Bill realized Tallulah was staring at him with a questioning look on her face, as if checking this was part of his Plan. Bill shook his head blankly. Tallulah gave the black knight a sideways look, shrugged, and climbed up onto one of the desks.

"You heard the man," she yelled, stamping her foot. "Drop your weapons!"

The knight in black cleared his throat, looking somewhat taken aback. "Excuse me," he said, letting his sword fall to his side. "But *I'm* robbing this bank."

Tallulah dropped out of sight for a moment. Seconds later, a knight in yellow armour clambered onto the desk beside her. "No, *I'm* robbing this bank!" he shouted.

"I'm robbing the bank!" called another, climbing up beside him.

"I am!" came a shout from far down the aisle.

"And me!"

"Me too! And him!"

The room filled with the enthusiastic shouts of the knights. The grey knight standing over Bill gave him a fierce look, then, waving forward the other grey knights who lined the walls, roared, "Charge!" and leapt towards the middle of the room.

Bill suddenly felt warm breath at his feet, and when he looked down there was the antelope, clutching a set of keys in its mouth and blinking.

"Hello, 'lope!" pealed Phly, stroking its ears fondly. "What nice jingly keys!"

"Thank you," said Bill, giving the antelope a quick pat before ducking down to unlock himself.

The antelope blinked at him with a look that suggested such things were beneath it, then trotted over to the old woman, and nudged her ankle.

Bill tried throwing the keys, but they skittered out under the feet of a grey knight, who toppled to the ground with a crash.

"Good shot," said the old woman, rescuing the keys and slipping the shackle off her ankle. She passed them on down the row, and within minutes, hundreds of uniformed bank workers had unchained themselves.

The battle in the centre aisle, meanwhile, was not going well. The rusty blades of the many-coloured knights were no match for the bright new swords of Silva's guards. Fernando kept trying to push his daughter out of the way of any approaching sword, usually whirling her into the path of another one. Whistler had fared rather better for a time, by casting off his blue cloak and pretending to be a horrifying demon, but once the grey knights realized that even if he was a horrifying demon, he was one without any weapons or magical powers, he had stopped being frightening. He was now cowering under a desk, whistling in panic. The black knight who had declared the robbery in the first place, meanwhile, was still standing in the doorway holding a grey knight hostage and looking a bit miffed at having his robbery hijacked.

Bill stuck his head out from under the desk, and decided that it would probably be a good idea to be somewhere else. Phly had wrapped herself around his leg for safety, so as he stepped carefully over the fallen knight, he lifted his sword out of the way to make sure the elph didn't hurt herself. The antelope trotted in front of him, 'eef'ing softly in the chaos, and suddenly a great cheer rang through the room.

"Sir Bill!" yelled Tallulah, enthusiastically kicking a grey knight in the head.

Bill stared, bewildered, at the seething crowd of knights, who had all stopped fighting, and turned to look his way. Then he looked at the sword he was holding up, and, with a quick glance over his shoulder, realized he was leading forward an army of grey-suited workers, all waving their rubber stamps, pens and hole punches in the air.

"Reinforcements!" yelled Tallulah.

With a roar the bank workers surged forward and joined the fray, leaping onto the backs of the grey knights and rubber-stamping them into submission. Grey suit jackets were flung in their faces, blinding them with matted purple fur. Hole punches clanged against swords, making small, oddly-shaped dents in the blades. The long chain which had pinned them to their desks was now being wound around the legs of their guards, yanking their feet from under them and sending them crashing to the carpet.

Bill was swept along in the tide of jubilant workers, and found himself in the thick of the battle, still holding the sword up above his head out of the way. His arm was grasped by a firm hand, and he looked up to find Fernando grinning at him.

"Excellent Plan, Sir Bill," he shouted above the noise. "What do you propose next?"

"Um… running away?" said Bill feebly, as a grey knight fell across his foot, armour stamped all over with brightly coloured Xs.

"Retreat and regroup, of course!" cried Fernando, dragging him through the throng, Phly still clinging to his leg. Tallulah waved at him from on top of a desk, and leapt into the crowd to follow them, hauling a moaning Whistler with her.

All five emerged from the heaving mass of people at once, and found the antelope already standing in the open doorway, blinking. Bill stopped to catch his breath, but found himself suddenly enveloped in something warm, fluffy, and very familiar.

"Thought you might miss it," said Tallulah with a grin, tugging great loops of his scarf from the bag at her feet.

Bill buried his nose in the warm wool, not minding that the scratchy gold stripe was tickling his chin, or that it was a bit dusty from its time in the rafters of The Three Kings' Heads.

"Thank you," he said.

Tallulah grinned again, then grabbed the end of the scarf and pulled him towards the open doorway. They were almost out in the open air, when Bill heard a sudden rattle of chains. A moment later the ornate portcullis came crashing down, millimetres from the end of his nose.

"Pilf!" shouted the princess, as they staggered backwards. Bill was still checking all of him was still attached, including Phly, who was now gripping his leg very tightly and shuddering musically, when a sharp whistle of alarm made him look up. A grey knight was emerging from the shadows, his sword raised to attack.

Bill froze, panicked, but Fernando leapt forward, tearing the sword from Bill's hand and hurling himself at the knight.

"No one tries to drop a portcullis on my daughter's head and gets away with it!" he shouted.

"Go, Dad!" whooped Tallulah, keeping hold of the end of Bill's scarf and plunging back into the battling crowd of knights, guards and bank clerks. Casting a quick look at King Fernando fending off the guard, Bill hurried after her, sidestepping fists and blades as best he could. When they staggered out at the other side, he saw where she was heading: a narrow doorway, leading to a set of stairs.

"But this takes us back up," he protested, as she hauled him up the winding stairs, Whistler and the antelope close on their heels.

"So?" said Tallulah. "There's got to be a window or something we can jump out of. What's in here?"

They raced out of the staircase, and skidded to a halt. Rows of desks stretched off into the distance, torches casting dim light over the bent heads of the quietly whispering workers. Hundreds of pale faces turned their way. The whispering stopped. The workers began to stand up.

Behind them, they could hear echoing feet coming up the narrow staircase, and the heads of several grey knights appeared.

"Come on!" Tallulah shouted, and sprinted into the room, her heavy boots thudding on the pale blue carpet.

"But it's a dead end!" Bill gasped breathlessly as he stumbled after her, wishing she would let go of the end of the scarf.

They pelted down the aisle, Phly finally releasing Bill's leg and jumping onto Whistler's back to be carried along. The antelope ran on ahead, as the pale sea of faces on either side began to close in on them. Close behind, he could hear the clanking of the grey knights' armour as they gave chase. Not far ahead, Bill could make out the last desk at the back of the room, and a silver-haired figure rising to his feet.

"No running in the bank! Stop!" shouted Owen Silva, holding up his ringed hands.

They slowed to a dead halt in front of the desk, Tallulah wrinkling her nose at Silva. "Nice cape," she said sarcastically.

"In the elegance stakes, my dear, you're hardly in a position to talk," he said with a smile. "Guards, take them to the… Oooooof!"

Without warning, Bill felt a crushing tightness around his neck, and was knocked onto his knees. Whistler had been running down the aisle looking over his shoulder at the grey knights who had chased them up the stairs, and had charged right into the scarf strung between Bill and Tallulah, as if it were the finishing tape in a rather violent marathon. He flew into the air, smacking directly into

Silva and knocking him flat onto his desk. Phly soared over their heads with a squeal, hitting the soft velvet of the purple curtain under the portraits, and disappearing.

Whistler kneeled up. "So sorry," he said, straightening the circlet on Silva's ruffled hair. "Very clumsy of me."

"Where's Phly gone?" Bill said, scrambling to his feet and looking round wildly, as the grey guards drew even closer.

"Through there!" said Tallulah, pointing at the back wall. Poking her head out from behind the purple curtain, the elph was smiling excitedly; at her feet stood the antelope.

"Come and look in here!" sang Phly.

Bill sprinted round the desk, and saw that the purple curtain covered the entrance to a very small, entirely round room with a shiny silver floor and a strange, clean smell. As he, Tallulah and Whistler raced inside, the curtain fell back behind them, and with a click and a whirr, a series of very bright electric lights went on.

Blinking in the brightness, Bill looked up, and saw that the lights stretched up in narrowing lines above them, as if they were in a tunnel that went upwards. Then he almost lost his balance, as the floor began to move, rising up through the tunnel like a lift. The purple curtain disappeared, and the angry shouts of the guards were suddenly cut off.

Up above, there was another loud whirring noise. A line of darkness appeared, forming a crescent, then a half-moon, then a black circle above their heads, getting larger and larger as the floor moved up to meet it.

Cold air blew down from above, and Bill was just about to ask why he could see stars, when the floor reached the mouth of the tunnel. Far below were the lights of the castle city, and with a start Bill realized they were at the top of the clock tower in the centre, with the pointed witch's hat for a roof. Peeping over the edge, he could see that the hat had some sort of hinge, and it had flipped open to let the floor out.

The platform rose a few more feet above the top of the tower, then gave the tiniest of shudders, and stopped. To Bill's absolute horror, the shiny surface beneath their feet suddenly turned to silvery liquid.

But instead of falling away from under their feet, the liquid began to move, and slide, and rise up all around them like a huge bowl. The lights were slowly blocked out, and then the stars began to disappear, and it grew darker and darker inside the bowl as it closed over their heads.

Bright electric lights, like the ones in the tunnel, flashed on, and Bill discovered that they were now standing inside a huge silver egg. He tentatively put out a hand, but the liquid surface seemed to have solidified, and now felt cool, like metal.

"Wow," said Tallulah.

"Hello, egg!" sang Phly.

"Eef," said the antelope, quietly.

Bill said nothing, and stared at Whistler. The alien was standing close to the gently curving wall, stroking its surface with a broad smile on his damp, grey face. He let a soft whistle escape from his gills, as a faint whining sound began to grow in the background.

"Crew," he said proudly, "I suggest you find something to hold onto. We are about to go on a trip."

Bill was about to ask what exactly he was supposed to hold onto inside a giant silver egg with totally bare walls, but the words never got out of his mouth. The whining noise built to a roar, and with a massive bang, the egg shot up into the sky at terrifying speed.

Chapter Eight

The Egg

... in which Bill discovers a new way to travel

Bill found himself pressed against the curved walls of the egg, pinned there by the incredible force that was driving them upwards. He tried to move, but there seemed to be hundreds of invisible hands holding him down, grinding him into the cool wall. Phly was squashed beside him, flattened out like a green cushion with very wide eyes. Tallulah was spread-eagled on the opposite wall, looking in alarm at her hair as it spread out in a flat halo around her. Even the antelope looked a little anxious, its slender legs quivering as they began to bend to fit the curved wall.

"Must... adjust... gravity..." said Whistler in a strangled voice, sliding himself with difficulty along the wall and running his bony hands along the silver surface.

Bill's nose appeared to be trying to spread itself out across his face to reach his ears. Then, very slowly, the invisible hands began to let go. He could breathe again and wiggle his fingers. In fact, after being so firmly pressed against the wall, he felt strangely floaty.

With a gasp, he realized that the floating sensation wasn't just in his head. He was slowly lifting off from the silver wall, drifting towards the middle of the egg. His scarf waved gently in the air as if it were swimming; springs of hair fluttered round his face like strands of seaweed. The others were floating too, the antelope latching onto the leg of Whistler's dungarees with its teeth to stop itself from rising too high. Tallulah reached out to catch Phly, but instead sent her spinning with a soft chiming sound towards the ceiling, where she bounced and tumbled slowly back again, giggling. Bill closed his eyes and let himself drift, weightless, a balloon on a breezy day...

With a thud, he hit the floor.

A chorus of tinkles, 'eef's and groaning noises followed.

"Sorry, rather fiddly controls," said Whistler, swiping at the wall with a rueful smile. "Should be all right now, though."

"Whistler, mate," said Tallulah, wrinkling up her nose as she rubbed a sore knee. "What the pilfing flink *is* this thing?"

"This," said the alien, spreading his arms out and smiling proudly, "is a Mercuroid. Probably an old Type 41; later versions are a little more sophisticated. Auto-grav, chairs, windscreen wipers, that sort of thing."

"Ooh! There are others like this?" cooed Phly, her enormous dark eyes reflecting the silvery sheen of the walls.

Whistler gave a satisfied little cough. "Hundreds. Of course, most of the ships in our main fleet are much more impressive."

Bill gazed at the shiny, shadowless curves of the egg, and thought that he'd be most impressed by being able to see a large door marked 'Exit'.

"Hang on," said Tallulah. "If this thing's from your layer of the universe, how did it get down to mine?"

"My world was taken over by the Great Spondozo and his Gatherers much as yours was," said Whistler, wiping his wrinkly head sadly. "This Mercuroid was probably an escape pod of sorts for your bank manager friend, Bill."

Bill was about to object that Owen Silva had kidnapped him and chained him to the floor, and he hadn't thought that was all that friendly, but the elph hopped up excitedly.

"Does that mean we're going to the centre of the universe to stop the Great Spondozo and free all the slaves now?"

Bill felt a rumble of worry in his stomach, but Whistler was shaking his head.

"No," he said. "The Great Spondozo is *down*, and we are most definitely going *up*. If you look just here," he went on, pointing at a completely blank piece of silvery wall, "you'll see the AND."

"The AND?" said Bill, staring at the blank wall.

"Antenmann's Navigational Destinator," said Whistler, beaming. "A totally unique piece of technology. Gregorius Antenmann realized, many years ago, that explorers like myself faced one particular difficulty: travelling between the layers was only possible when a hole at the bottom of one layer coincided with a hole at the top of the next. And since the layers all revolve and rotate and spin inside one another, it was impossible to predict when that might happen. Explorers spent years staring at holes in the ground, poised, waiting to jump in if they spotted anything passing below."

Tallulah sniggered, and Whistler broke off, looking hurt. "There were some who found our plight amusing," he said, coughing and looking at a point above her head. "Some even called for the League of Expeditioners to be disbanded. Then Antenmann cracked it: a navigational device, fitted to all transports, which automatically located the next connecting pair of holes."

"Ooh, clever," sang Phly, clapping her hands.

"Actually, the basic principle is remarkably simple," the alien said, giving Tallulah a condescending look. "The easiest explanation is a bucket with a hole in it. Fill the bucket with water, and the water will find its way through the hole."

Tallulah wrinkled her nose. "And how does it do that?"

Whistler cleared his throat. "Ah… well…"

"I thought you said we were going up?" sang Phly, frowning. "Water doesn't go up."

"No… you see, there isn't any actual water…" stuttered Whistler, coughing again.

"And what would happen if there was more than one hole in the bucket?" said Tallulah.

"Stop!" Whistler said loudly, holding up his hands and whistling sharply through his gills. "There isn't a bucket, there isn't any water, and you don't need to know how it works. It just does, all right?"

From somewhere outside there was a thump, and a loud grinding noise, as if the egg was scraping against something. They jolted and bucked, then carried on as before.

"Most of the time, anyway," Whistler added, steadying himself against the wall and trying to look nonchalant.

"Um," said Bill, wondering at the amount of time it seemed be taking, since he'd always assumed that spaceships were a lot faster than cars. "So... if we're not going to the Great Spondozo's hiding place in the centre of the universe, where exactly *are* we going?"

"Well, in theory, anywhere you want," said Whistler.

"Can I go home?" sang Phly, hopping on one leg. "I like home."

"Hey, what about freeing all the slaves?" said Tallulah, prodding her with a grubby finger.

The elph put her fuzzy head on one side. "Can I go home after that?"

"I suppose I ought to check my dad's all right," said Tallulah. "And all those knights might come in handy. We'd probably better stop back at my place before we invade, if that's all right with everyone. Anything you need to pick up from home, Bill?"

Bill bit his lip, and looked at the floor. He didn't think there was much a small coastal town in South Wales could offer to defeat an evil genius. Except perhaps his parents, who were probably so angry by now they'd take on the Great Spondozo all by themselves. If he went home, they certainly wouldn't be letting him out of their sight any time soon.

He felt a little flutter of relief at the thought of being safely banished to his bedroom. His blurry reflection in the silver floor looked back at him, all wool and springs of hair. Home was where he belonged: home, where the floors didn't melt and turn into spaceships, where there were no people chasing him with swords, and where no one ever made the mistake of asking him to do the Planning. If he just asked Whistler to drop him off at the end of his street, it would probably be better for everyone.

Not much a small coastal town in South Wales could offer... Tallulah lived in a world where wars happened every day, and they hadn't been able to resist the Great Spondozo. Whistler's people could build liquid ships and Navigational Destinators, and the Great Spondozo had taken their world over too. South Wales wouldn't stand a chance. The little flutter of relief went away, and left him feeling slightly sick, and cold. It didn't matter how hopeless the silvery Bill in the floor looked. It was far too late for him just to go home.

Bill opened his mouth to say his world couldn't provide too many real knights, but that he would stay and fight, or at least try to, but Whistler was shaking his head again.

"No, no, no. I said *in theory* we could go anywhere. Antenmann's dream was a map of all the layers, which could be downloaded into the Navigational Destinator. Then you could just look at the list and choose where you wanted to go. But, of course, until we'd travelled to all the different layers, we couldn't make the map..."

"And until you made the map, you couldn't travel to all the different layers," said Tallulah, rolling her eyes. "Thought you said this Antenmann bloke was a genius?"

Whistler puffed out his narrow chest, looking offended. "He was a genius. If the last expedition of the Brian IV hadn't ended in tragedy, he'd probably have completed the map by now." Whistler pressed his hand to the shiny symbol embroidered on his front pocket, and looked at some distant point with teary eyes. "In his absence, explorers like myself shall continue his fine works, until the map is completed..."

"Easy with the hero-worship, Whistler. I'm sure he was a great guy," said Tallulah, stumbling as another scraping noise sounded from outside the egg. "I just wish he'd remembered the concept of steering."

Then there was a small bing noise, like a microwave, and the faint whine of the Mercuroid's engines faded into silence.

"Aha! We've arrived," said Whistler.

"Where?" said Bill.

"No idea," said Whistler, waving his hand vaguely over the wall.

Where his hand had passed, a small circular hole appeared in the silver. Bill stepped back in alarm, thinking that the egg was melting away around them just as it had grown, but the circle widened until it was about the size of a dinner plate, then stopped, forming a sort of porthole.

The view was disappointing. There seemed to be nothing outside at all; just darkness.

"Is it bedtime?" asked Phly.

"Maybe we're still in the hole," murmured Tallulah, reaching out and poking the porthole to check there was something still between her and the outside. The invisible glass rippled outwards, like a pool of water, then stilled again.

"Possible, possible," muttered Whistler, delving into his pocket and producing the Knowletron. As he lifted it up, something bright flashed past the porthole, very fast. There was a faint pinging sound, and the egg quivered slightly.

"What was that?" said Bill, drawing back a little.

"Oh, probably just some kind of weather phenomenon," said Whistler, shrugging as there was another flash, ping, quiver. "Hailstorm, perhaps?"

But the pinging continued, getting faster, and louder, till the whole egg was juddering. The antelope 'eef'ed loudly, and Bill realized the walls of the Mercuroid were now covered in small knobbly lumps pointing inwards, as if it had some kind of metallic measles. More lumps were appearing by the second.

"Ooh! Bumpy," sang Phly, putting her hand out to the egg wall, and squeaking as she pulled it back quickly. "Hot," she mumbled, putting a finger in her mouth.

Bill agreed. His face was sweaty, the soles of his shoes had gone oddly sticky, and there was definitely steam rising from one silvery wall.

"Er… Whistler?" said Tallulah, putting her face close to the bumps, and jumping as a new dent appeared right in front of her nose.

"Yes, well, I think that's enough exploring of this particular layer, crew," coughed Whistler, hopping up and down and blowing on his fingers as he tapped urgently at the hot silver. "Just need to initiate the departure sequence…"

The engines began to whine, sounding rather unhappy about it, and with a shudder, the Mercuroid took off again. There was still steam billowing from one side of the egg, and if anything, it was getting hotter.

"Is it supposed to be doing that?" said Tallulah, pointing at the steam and sounding more nervous than cross.

Whistler wiped an anxious hand over his small head. "Probably just a rupture in the... er... carmologous matrix... causing a outflux of... mimbinium..."

"Which means?"

Whistler cleared his throat and looked apologetic. "I think it means we're going to crash."

Around them the egg groaned, as if agreeing. The whine of the engines grew more strained. Bill shut his eyes tightly, and held his breath.

Without warning, the shuddering stopped. The engines stopped whining. Steam stopped pouring from the silvery walls, and the temperature dropped to that of a reasonably sunny day.

The egg went bing.

"Please remain seated, your journey is almost completed," said a soft, melodic voice.

Bill opened his eyes. Tallulah, Phly and the antelope were staring at the ceiling, looking for the source of the voice.

"Hello?" sang Phly, waving at the walls.

"What's happening?" said Bill, peering at the porthole. The invisible barrier that formed the window was a little bumpy, showing the outside world at odd angles like a fairground mirror, but the picture was clear enough.

Space. Black skies, speckled with stars. A strange purple glow, surrounding the Mercuroid. And planets. Lots of planets.

There was a low whistle from behind him, and Bill looked up to see Whistler gazing at the view with an odd look on his face.

"The rupture must have activated the homing device," he said, in a slightly strangled voice.

"Please remain seated, your journey is almost completed," said the voice again.

"Homing device? So… this is your home?" said Tallulah, watching, fascinated as the nearest planet drew closer. It shimmered silver, shining more brightly than the stars, and filling the screen so that it hardly looked as if there were a window there.

Whistler nodded wordlessly.

"Hooray!" yelled Phly, leaping up to smother the alien in a fuzzy hug.

"And we're not going to crash?" said Tallulah, a crooked grin creeping across her face.

Whistler shook his head. "Auto-docking net," he said, gesturing vaguely at the purple mist surrounding the egg.

"Nice one, matey," the princess said, punching the alien fondly on the arm.

Bill gave him a grateful smile, but Whistler went on staring out of the window at the planet below. Something swished past Bill's leg, and he looked down to see the antelope, blinking up at the alien with a curious expression.

"Please remain seated, your journey is almost

completed," the voice repeated. Then there was a faint humming noise, and the silvery image in the porthole glowed, as if someone was shining torches on the egg. With a small clink, the Mercuroid touched down, and melted away around them like ice under a hairdryer.

They had arrived in the most enormous room Bill had ever seen. It was so large he suspected that it might not even count as a room, since he could see no sign of a ceiling, or any walls: only a faint bluish light rising up from beneath them, and glowing down on them from above. Instead of leaving a flat disc of silver, as before, the Mercuroid had disappeared into the silvery floor, dissolving into it without any sign of a join. But even the floor wasn't really a floor; they were standing on a large circular podium, which extended downwards in a solid tube of silver, and although the other end of the tube was probably attached to something, Bill didn't feel too comfortable standing close enough to the edge to find out what. It was a little like standing on the end of a giant pencil lead.

"Landing platform," murmured Whistler, dusting himself down with rather shaky hands.

Bill stared out, and saw hundreds of other silver cylinders stretching out at intervals all around, some a little taller than theirs, some so low he could barely make them out in the bluish light. A faint, cool breeze blew into his eyes; there was a slightly sweet smell in the air, like custard creams. It was very still, very quiet, and the sheer size of the place after being inside the egg quite took his breath away.

The antelope's chocolatey eyes shone silver-blue as it delicately stepped to the edge of the podium to peer over the edge. Phly was kneeling down, staring at her reflection in the silvery floor, and trying to catch it doing something she wasn't. Even Tallulah was breathless with awe.

"Whistler, mate," she said eventually, sounding unusually honest. "This place is… it's just so…"

"Shiny," Phly finished for her, in a soft, sweet tone.

"Yeah," said Tallulah. "*Shiny.*"

The quiet stillness was broken by a whirring sound from above, and suddenly Bill found himself looking directly into what looked like an eye on a piece of string. A long silver cable had descended from somewhere above him, and dangling from the end was a short black cylinder capped with glass, like a camera lens, watching him closely. Four other eyes were hanging from above, pointing at the others.

"Um… Whistler?" stuttered Bill, but before he could go on, all five of them were suddenly bathed in soft purple light, flooding from the five lenses. The light felt strangely tingly, as if it had fingers and was running them over his skin to see what he felt like. It travelled from the top of his head down to his feet, catching the ticklish bit inside his elbow and making him gasp, and then went out.

"Unknown," said a nasal, robotic voice.

Bill bit his lip, wondering whether he was expected to answer.

"Unknown," said the voice again, this time coming from the lens in front of Tallulah.

"Same to you," said the princess, sticking out her tongue.

"Hello!" sang Phly, waving at the dangling lens in front of her.

"Unknown," said the voice.

The voice seemed to pause a long time over the antelope, as if uncertain quite what to make of it, while the small creature blinked impassively.

"Unknown," it said, at last.

Then it came to Whistler, and Bill realized that the alien was looking rather despondently at the floor, and very softly whistling through his gills.

"I'm really very sorry," he said in a quiet voice, avoiding their eyes.

The calm air was suddenly filled with a blaring siren, honking repeatedly, while the five lenses flashed red lights on and off.

"Quxynggrotly 227, you are under arrest for the contravention of section 54c, sub-section D22, of the Expeditioners' Handbook," said the robotic voice. "Sentence to be carried out immediately."

"Sentence?" said Tallulah, putting her hands on her hips. "Arrested? Whistler, what's going on?"

The alien didn't answer, but merely pointed upwards. Far above them, another silver cylinder exactly like the one they stood on was descending towards them, at such phenomenal speed that if it didn't stop soon, it would squash them flat. Instinctively, Bill closed his eyes and ducked down.

There was a whump, and a rush of cool air in his face. Bill opened one eye timidly, and looked up to see the base of the other silver tube hovering a few feet above his head, barely leaving room for Whistler to stand up. Surrounding the space between the two cylinders, circling them like a quiet tornado, spun a fine purple mist, which sparked dangerously.

"Life imprisonment," said the voice.

And all the lights went out.

Chapter Nine

The Interplanetary
Multi-Galactic
Peace Conference

... in which Bill makes a speech

Bill had caused many disasters during his life, but even
he had never done anything awful enough to get arrested.
Even so, he was fairly sure that a trial usually came before
a sentence of life imprisonment. In Whistler's case, that
seemed to have been forgotten. As he sat in the gloom,
with the only light coming from the sparking purple
whirlwind trapping them in their silver prison, Bill
guiltily wondered what on earth (or anywhere else, for
that matter) the alien could have done.

"Oi! Idiots!" yelled Tallulah, her voice echoing eerily
in the darkness. "You've made a mistake! He's your Lord
High Expeditioner!"

With a fizz and a hiss, the silver chamber suddenly
glowed orange. Bill turned to see Phly kneeling, a ball of
flame nestling in her cupped palms.

"At least we won't get cold," she sang, trying to sound

bright and dropping the fireball into the centre of the circle, where it burned as if there were twigs and sticks beneath it, not hard, bare silver.

"Hello-o!" shouted Tallulah, leaning forwards. "Is anyone listening to... ouch!" Her finger had touched the purple swirl, sending a shower of sparks into the air. "It *bit* me!" she said angrily, sucking her finger.

"Force field," came a quiet voice from the other side of the circle, followed by a long, damp sniff. "Can't be deactivated from inside."

Whistler's face was even more crumpled than usual, and by the flickering light of the elph's fire, Bill could see tears welling in his yellow eyes. He looked impossibly sad.

"Whistler? Are you poorly?" sang Phly. She swished over to him and rubbed her fuzzy head against his knee, but the alien gently pushed her away.

"Please don't," he said. "I don't deserve it. I've done a terrible thing, and now..."

With a staticky hum, all the lights in the vast room flicked back on, dazzling them. When his vision had cleared, Bill realized they were no longer alone. Standing on top of the nearest silver cylinder was a figure who looked an awful lot like Whistler. It had a grey, shrivelled-looking head, wore a pair of yellow dungarees, and looked rather harassed.

"Excuse me," said the figure, in a croaky, but undoubtedly female voice. "So sorry to interrupt..."

"Hello!" sang Phly brightly.

Tallulah tapped her sharply on the head. "Don't be nice to them, they're the ones who trapped us here!"

she said, glaring at the alien.

"An automated response, I'm afraid, due to our high security status," said the alien woman, wringing her hands apologetically. "And you are rather late."

"Late?" said Tallulah, rudely. "Late for what?"

"For the Interplanetary Multi-Galactic Peace Conference, of course. Naturally, we're having to take rather extreme precautions to keep so many arrivals a secret. Can't afford to let a single spy slip through our net. Of course, when we realized who you had with you…"

Tallulah's face broke into a grin, and she gave Whistler a punch on the arm. "Being a celebrity has its uses, eh, Whistle-boy?"

Bill got the strong impression that the alien woman's smile was actually directed at the antelope, and from Whistler's vague whistle of unease, he was fairly sure Whistler thought so too. But the woman was continuing.

"Most of the other delegates arrived yesterday, and the opening banquet is already underway – so if you could just name your ambassador, I'll take you along to your quarters. Obviously, after this unfortunate incident, I'll make sure you're placed in our finest suite."

"Oh," said Phly, giggling. "I think there's been a…"

"Terrible delay in our arrival," cut in Tallulah loudly, stepping in front of Phly and clamping a hand over her fuzzy nose. "Awful weather. And the traffic? Don't get me started. But we're here now. To represent… er…" She looked around wildly for inspiration, then gave Bill a wink. "To represent the planet Skarf. This is Bill, our ambassador."

She drew back and gestured at Bill, nudging him with her foot. Bill struggled to his feet and gazed nervously upwards.

The alien woman eyed him dubiously. "Aren't you a little short for an ambassador?" she said.

Bill coughed, and tried to look official and important.

"Very well," she croaked, and tapped the shiny symbol on the front of her dungarees. The purple mist sparkled silver for a moment, then vanished. With a faint swooshing sound, the entire silver tube they were standing on began to sink downwards, gathering speed as it descended, and wafting springs of Bill's hair upwards.

"See you at the banquet," called the woman, nodding at them from far above, and waving until she disappeared from view.

A short time later, Bill found himself sitting in the most comfortable chair he'd ever had the pleasure of putting his bottom on. It was soft, warm and slightly furry, like sitting in the arms of a large and strangely welcoming cat.

The rest of their suite was no less perfect. The silver floor of the huge tube they had been standing on had detached itself, and glided into another cylindrical tower, this one with walls and doors, before dissolving seamlessly into the floor. In the silvery walls of their round chamber were five circular openings, leading to five small but luxurious bedrooms. Best of all was the main door. It was made of the same silvery liquid as the Mercuroid, and instead of swinging open, when you approached it cascaded like a waterfall and merged with the floor, rising up again in a silvery tide once you had passed. Since their arrival, Phly had done nothing but step forward to make it flow downwards, and then jump back as it surged up, clapping her hands and jingling with delight.

None of this distracted Bill from his misery. He had absolutely no idea what might be expected of a delegate at a peace conference, but chances were he wouldn't be very good at it. Worse still, laid out on the bed for him to wear had been a long silvery smock of scratchy material that looked, in all honesty, like a bridesmaid's dress. Whistler had pulled it over Bill's head on top of his ordinary clothes, insisting that it was a formal uniform, and was now fussing around at Bill's feet, adjusting the hem. Everywhere Bill looked, he could see reflections of himself, pink with embarrassment.

"It'll be fine!" said Tallulah breezily, dangling her legs over the arm of a furry chair and grinning. "I had to come up with something. And this way, we get to stay in really swanky rooms, go to a banquet… you get to wear that lovely dress…"

"If it's going to be so easy, why didn't you say *you* were the ambassador for the planet Skarf?" said Bill.

"What, after you did such a great job of being Sir Bill? You're a natural."

"But I don't even know what an ambassador does," he protested.

"Diplomacy," mumbled Whistler unhelpfully, through a mouthful of pins.

Bill frowned at the grey wrinkled head below. The look of terrible sadness that had lined Whistler's face in the purple prison had vanished, and every time Bill tried to mention it, somehow the subject seemed to change very quickly.

"Whistler," he began in a low voice. "About what you said earlier… Ow!"

A sharp, stabbing pain hit his leg.

"So sorry," said Whistler, holding up a pin with a streak of red at its tip. "How clumsy of me."

Bill's eyes met Whistler's, and the look in them was not entirely friendly.

"Whistler?" said Bill, taken aback.

"If I were you, Bill," said the alien coolly, "I'd be worrying about the banquet. This is going to be a formal occasion: the slightest breach of etiquette could give you away."

Bill swallowed, the nervousness creeping back.

"Just don't talk with your mouth full," said Tallulah.

"Remember to use the right fork," added Whistler.

"How will I know which is the right fork?" said Bill.

"And don't offend anyone," said Tallulah, "or they might declare war on you."

"At a peace conference?" said Bill.

"Just be yourself," sang Phly, giving a spring of his hair an encouraging tug.

Bill looked at her hopeful little face, and thought to himself that that was possibly the worst advice ever uttered. But before he could protest further, a sloshing noise interrupted them, and he looked up to see the smiling, crinkly face of the alien in the yellow dungarees.

"Ready, ambassador?" she said, bowing slightly.

Bill took a deep breath and stood up, trying to ignore

the way the smock itched and stuck out around his neck at funny angles.

"Excellent," said the alien woman, giving him a sideways smile as she headed out into the corridor that made Bill feel even more self-conscious. Even with Whistler's adjustments, the smock was still too long, and the sleeves kept dropping down over his hands; if he got through the evening without tripping on it, he thought, it would be a miracle. He shuffled after her, with Tallulah, Phly and Whistler following. The antelope trotted after them, but Tallulah shooed it back into the room.

"You'll only get underfoot," she scolded, as the door surged up behind them.

Like everything else they had seen so far, the corridors were shiny and silver, with soft bluish lights glowing upwards from the floor. Although he had to admit it looked impressive, all the silver was starting to annoy Bill. Everywhere he looked, he saw reflections of himself and the others, or reflections of their reflections, as if they were being followed by an army of shadowy versions of themselves. Even more irritating were the liquid doors. Although they sloshed obediently into the floor at their approach, and swished back up again behind them, it looked to Bill a little like they were showing off.

As they followed the alien woman through the nineteenth liquid door, Bill found himself stepping out into another vast room whose floors and ceilings were too far away to see. The floor they had been walking down continued on beyond the corridor, however: a thin ribbon of silver stretching away across a bottomless chasm. Bill gulped.

"Now, just a little reminder," croaked the alien woman, smiling at Bill. "When the Ambassador of Quxyng enters the chamber, stand up and bow three times to the left, three times to the right, and three times to the middle. Don't touch the Ambassador for Gendinah, its skin is poisonous. And when you make your speech, do it nice and loud; even with headphones some of the older delegates are a little deaf."

"A speech?" whispered Bill, turning pale. Public speaking was not just something he was bad at; it was something he simply couldn't do.

(The pattern had been set at the age of six, when, to his embarrassment, he had been cast as Father Christmas' wife in the school Christmas play, because he had the prettiest hair.

"Good night, Mary, I'll see you on Boxing Day," Father Christmas was supposed to say.

And Bill was supposed to reply, "I'll put your slippers by the fire, for when you get home."

Bill had known exactly what his line was. By the morning of the performance, he'd repeated it to himself so many times that whenever his parents asked him a question, such as, "Would you like some more cereal?" or, "Have you put your lunch in your bag?" he could only reply, "I'll put your slippers by the fire, for when you get home," like a robot.

But once he was on the stage, something happened to his voice.

"See you on Boxing Day," Father Christmas said.

"I'll put your slippers by the fire, for when you get home," Bill replied, in his head.

But his tongue said nothing. Father Christmas stared at him in confusion. Rudolph the reindeer poked him in the side. The audience began to murmur and whisper.

"Aww, he's forgotten his line," a sympathetic voice said.

"No, I haven't," said Bill in his head, but Mrs Hotchkiss clapped loudly and shooed them off the stage. The audience giggled and applauded, and afterwards everyone said how lovely the play was, and how it didn't matter that Mrs Christmas forgot her line, and all the time Bill still couldn't get his mouth to work to say that he hadn't forgotten it at all.

"He'll grow out of it," his dad always said. But he hadn't. At least, not in time.)

Before Bill could turn and make a run for it, a whisper of wind ruffled through his hair, and he realized the silver ribbon was moving, swooping downwards and carrying them with it. Below them, he could see what looked like a circular stadium, apparently suspended in mid-air. Tiers of seating ran around the edge: in the centre, where the pitch ought to be, were hundreds of tables, spread out across a purple carpet.

As the arena loomed closer, Bill realized it was filled with people – if 'people' was the right word for such a bizarre collection of beings. There were plenty of Quxynggrotlys, their brightly-coloured dungarees making them stand out in the crowd, but their shrivelled heads looked positively ordinary next to the strange assortment of creatures below. There were things with big heads, things with four heads, and some things that didn't seem to have heads at all, but an excessive number of legs. Some of the ambassadors, all of whom seemed to be sitting in the top tier, were so vast that the silvery smock which was dwarfing Bill had to be worn as a sort of bracelet; others had disappeared in its folds, and were representing the views of their people from a bundle on the floor.

Bill had just noticed a surprising number of antelopes dotted among the crowds, when an amplified voice echoed in his ears.

"Please welcome Bill, ambassador for Skarf," said the voice.

His feet touched purple carpet, and as the silvery walkway fell away to nothingness behind him, a faint smattering of polite applause drifted up from the mass of beings below.

"Hello!" sang Phly, waving madly.

"Well, aren't you the popular one," murmured Tallulah in his ear, giving him a sly wink.

Bill swallowed nervously as millions of eyes (most of which were attached to a single yellow blob in the middle of the crowd) fixed upon him. Tentatively, he lifted his hand in a timid salute, waving the overlong silver sleeve. The faint applause dwindled away to nothing.

"This way, ambassador," said their wrinkly guide, grabbing Bill's sleeve and leading him off to the left. "Guests down to the lower floor, please."

Bill stumbled along after her, looking helplessly over his shoulder as the others were guided to a table on the lower level. Phly waved encouragingly, and Tallulah gave him a quick thumbs up. Whistler was busy basking in the attention, nodding graciously at the other guests.

Moments later, Bill was seated in the uppermost tier, with some rather peculiar neighbours. On his right sat a tall, hairy woman whose entire face appeared to be flaking off in large snowy chunks, and whose silver smock was speckled with white. In a bowl to his left was a squirming nest of tendrils, that looked to Bill alarmingly like his mum's spaghetti a la Monday, which was always covered in a mystery sauce made from Sunday lunch leftovers.

Bill drew his smock around him tightly, so as not to accidentally drop it in any of the brown goo that was oozing from the bowl of spaghetti, and accidentally nudged the arm of the woman to his right, sending a flurry of bits of skin into the air.

"Oh... sorry," he said, hastily.

"You're late," said the woman, in a dry, raspy voice.

"I know," said Bill, nervously.

"You've missed the banquet," she added, scratching her head and flicking chunks of scalp at him from under her fingernails.

"Er... really?" said Bill.

"Because you're late," she repeated, staring at him with crusty eyes.

"Yes," said Bill, starting to feel a little warm around the ears, and tugging at his scarf under the scratchy frock to loosen it. "I'm really very sorry about that..."

He shrank back as the woman leaned towards him.

"Ah, I don't blame you," she said, cackling and showing a row of brown, decaying teeth. "Quxynggrotlys are rotten cooks. I'm Trinkle, by the way. Ambassador for the Republic of Tring."

"Oh," said Bill, relieved. "I'm Bill. From… er… Skarf. Pleased to meet you."

He held out his hand to shake hers, and regretted it instantly, as several layers of crispy dry skin flaked away under his grasp. Pulling his hand back, he wiped it quickly on the smock, then recoiled as the spaghetti a la Monday on his left made a sudden bubbling noise. Brownish-yellow froth oozed from somewhere inside the coiled tendrils, and began to seep over the edge of its bowl.

"Don't mind the ambassador for Kittipi, he's just digesting himself," said Trinkle, with a dry cackle. "If you're peckish, you can help yourself to a bit of him."

She leaned over Bill, showering tiny bits of herself over the squirming bowl like salt, and plucked a tendril from the nest. It went on writhing between her fingers, oozing yellow slime, as she opened her mouth and lowered it in.

"No, really, I'm not hungry," murmured Bill, putting a hand to his stomach and feeling distinctly queasy.

As he did so, the lights in the arena dimmed to a pale glow.

"Aha," Trinkle rasped. "*Speech* time."

Bill moaned softly, as the amplified voice that had announced his arrival echoed out across the arena.

"Ladies and Gentlemen, Fluids and Gases, and, in case you made it after all, the Invisimen of Lexia 12, welcome to Quxyng's first Interplanetary Multi-Galactic Peace Conference."

Quiet applause rippled across the arena.

"The Organisational Committee would like to

apologize for any inconvenience our security restrictions may have caused," the voice went on, "but secrecy is paramount. You are all here at great personal risk. Your very presence in this room places you in grave danger. Let us dare to hope that the unities forged today will lead us to a safer future."

There was more applause, though Bill couldn't see much to clap about.

"To begin proceedings, please welcome the ambassador for Daarm, Krevitz Laluong."

On the opposite side of the arena, a spotlight appeared, flooding yellow light down on a baggy-skinned bald man who looked rather like a giant deflated baby. There was a fizz of static, then with a flicker a huge image of the bald man's face appeared, hundreds of metres wide, hovering in the air above the arena.

The crowd clapped again, as the baby-man on the screen nodded and smiled. Then he opened his mouth, and Bill shivered all over. The man didn't even seem to have said anything, but Bill's ears seemed filled up with silent noise. He could feel his eyeballs tingling, and his teeth vibrated inside his mouth.

Trinkle grabbed his arm, as Bill shook his head, opening and closing his mouth helplessly. She tapped the side of her head, and Bill saw she was wearing a very chunky pair of headphones, made of tubular steel that curved in a band across the top of her head, and then coiled up like a snail-shell at the ears. Bill looked around, and saw that everyone was wearing them. Even the spaghetti a la Monday had reached out a tendril, and tugged a pair into its bowl.

"Translator headphones," Trinkle rasped in his ear, unhooking a pair from under Bill's chair and handing them to him.

Bill slid the headphones onto his head with difficulty, the springy curls of his hair covering his ears and threatening to make them slip off again. But the fizzing tingle disappeared at once, and was replaced by a low, muffled voice.

It wasn't easy to follow what the man was saying: he was using a lot of long words, and the headphones kept sliding down around Bill's neck, leaving him trying to make sense of odd half-sentences like, "... determining factors which may legitimize the usage of..." and, "... are increasing exponentially during the time that...". He was about to give up entirely, when he heard the word "Gatherers".

Sitting up straight, he strained to hear the rest, but the huge image of the baby-man was fading, and the crowd broke out into more polite applause.

"Thank you," boomed the amplified voice. "Next to speak, we have Ambassador Hish of Snee."

The spotlight swung over to another part of the arena, and with a flicker the vast image of a slick-skinned blue-grey figure appeared before them. Bill was still struggling to keep up with all that was being said, but "Gatherers" were mentioned again, swiftly followed by something about "fighting the Great Spondozo".

At this, there was more applause, much louder than before. Bill let his headphones slide down around his neck, and tugged on the sleeve of Trinkle's smock.

"They're talking about the Great Spondozo?" he

said, in a loud whisper.

Trinkle slipped off her headphones.

"Of course," she rasped, "that's what we're here for, isn't it?"

Bill tried not to choke as she let out a dusty sigh. "Tring was taken over three years ago. Couldn't put up much of a fight on our own. Two Gatherer patrols, that was all it took. How long has Skarf been occupied?"

Bill barely heard the question: he was too busy gazing at the silver-smocked ambassadors. There were hundreds of them, representing hundreds of worlds...

"Everyone here," said Bill, feeling slightly breathless, "their worlds have been taken over the Great Spondozo, too?"

"This isn't all of them," Trinkle said, scratching a scabby patch on her chin. "Just the ones who weren't too scared to come."

Bill's mouth fell slightly open as he stared at the crowds. Whistler had talked about an evil genius taking over the universe, layer by layer, but Bill hadn't thought about those other worlds too much. Whistler had mentioned a resistance movement, too, but he certainly hadn't described anything like this. Bill allowed himself a little smile at the thought of Tallulah's grand talk of blowing up the Great Spondozo and freeing all the slaves. It was a hopeless plan, always had been – but it didn't matter now. Now they could leave it to people who knew what they were doing, and he could stand at the back handing out swords, or something equally helpful, till the difficult bits were over.

He settled back in his seat, immensely relieved, but

suddenly the room seemed very bright.

"Ambassador Bill of Skarf," said the announcer, and Bill realized with horror that the spotlight was now on him. The crowd applauded as a massive reproduction of his face appeared above them.

Bill swallowed, and cleared his throat. The sound echoed around the room. He tried to take a deep breath, but his chest felt oddly squeezed, as if his jumper had suddenly shrunk three sizes.

The clapping, he realized, had stopped. The vast room was silent, waiting for him to speak.

Bill opened his mouth, and said, in an odd, garbled voice that sounded nothing like his own, and without remotely meaning to, "I'll put your slippers by the fire, for when you get home."

If the room had been quiet before, the silence that echoed through the arena was a kind of reverse sound, as if a vacuum cleaner had sucked away even the tiniest bit of noise. Even Bill's own heartbeat, which had been thumping madly in his chest, seemed to have dwindled to nothing. He held his breath, closed his eyes, and thought to himself that if he lived through this moment, then his mother was right, and it was indeed impossible to die from embarrassment.

When he opened his eyes again, the spotlight was no longer on him, but instead of it moving to another ambassador, the lights across the whole arena slowly came back on. The silence continued.

Bill sank numbly back into his seat, and turned nervously to look at Trinkle. She was gazing at him with a stunned look on her scabby face. He scanned the speechless crowds below, and met a sea of blank faces, all looking equally astonished. At a table near the middle of the room, he could see one grubby pink face, one wrinkly grey one, and one fuzzy green one, and saw that they too looked dumbfounded by his performance.

"The banquet is over, please return to your quarters," said the announcer, in a dull, lifeless tone.

Without speaking, the crowds of people took off their headphones, slowly got to their feet (those that had them), and began to drift towards the edges of the arena, as the familiar silver walkways began unfurling themselves up in the sky.

Bill sighed heavily and stood up, slipping the headphones off his neck and dropping them miserably on the table. A small, metallic wasp crawled sleepily across the desk, making faint buzzing noises as if even it was disgusted with him. Bill nodded despondently at the wasp, agreeing with its verdict, and slowly shuffled away, feeling too wretched even to worry about tripping over his dress.

Chapter Ten

Unpopular

… in which Bill is both alone,
and the centre of attention

Back in their softly-lit room, Bill sat down in one of the furry chairs, and tried extremely hard not to cry. No one had spoken a word to him on the walk back from the banquet. Whistler had been a little peculiar since they'd arrived, but after that speech, everyone was ignoring him. Tallulah's blue eyes had stared right through him, as if she wanted to pretend he wasn't there, while Phly, who usually skipped and hummed as she walked, was oddly subdued, walking with her head bowed and avoiding his eyes. When they'd walked through the watery door, all three had gone directly to their bedrooms, and swished the doors closed behind them.

The antelope had been woken up by their return, and Bill looked hopelessly at it for some hint of a friendly face. But the shiny brown eyes simply blinked at him, and with a yawn, it fell asleep again. Bill was completely alone.

Wiping his nose on his scratchy silver sleeve, Bill wondered miserably what would happen to him now. He'd definitely done something wrong, but he wasn't sure what. His speech, if you could call it a speech, had probably given away the fact that he wasn't an ambassador, but no one had tried to stop them leaving, or to put them back in a tiny prison surrounded by a force field. No one had said anything at all. Perhaps they'd decided to give up on fighting the Great Spondozo, and were now all busy planning an attack on the planet Skarf. Perhaps mentioning the word 'slippers' at a peace conference was breaking some law no one had told him about, and in the morning they'd execute him.

With these vile possibilities circling in his head, Bill fell asleep in his chair, and had very bad dreams. In one, he was waist-deep in the gooey yolk of a boiled egg, and could only flail his arms as a huge, grinning Trinkle lowered a silver spoon towards him. In another, he was trying to swim through a thick lake of Lamb Beer, while giant red Xs fell from the sky like hailstones and threatened to hit him on the head. In the third, he was lying on his bed at home, with Whistler sticking a bony finger up his nose again, and Tallulah, Phly and the antelope standing over him, doubled over with laughter at the frightened look on his face.

Bill awoke with a start and realized that part of the last dream was true. There was something up his nose, wriggling and crawling and moving about. Bill sneezed, and the something flew out of his left nostril at such speed that it flew right across the room, hit the wall, and dropped to the floor with a tinny thunk. He sleepily walked over, and found a small metallic wasp, like the one that had crawled across the table in the arena. It was lying on its back, feebly cycling its tiny legs and making a grinding noise, like a clockwork mouse winding down.

Bill knelt and carefully picked it up by its iridescent wings. The wasp buzzed feebly at him, as if trying to tell him something, and Bill lifted it closer to his ear, feeling a little foolish. The buzzing grew louder, and beneath it Bill could just make out one word. "Follow," the wasp was saying, over and over again, like a scratched record.

"Follow you where?" said Bill, confused.

"Good morning, Bill," said a soft voice, right behind him.

Bill whirled round, and found Tallulah standing over him. At least, he was fairly sure it was Tallulah. She'd washed her face and brushed the tangles from her hair, and was wearing a silvery smock not unlike his own. Her clean, scrubbed face bore a soft, gentle smile, and her blue eyes were calm and sparkling. She looked, for the first time since they'd met, not just like a girl, but like a princess.

"Um... hello," said Bill, anxiously standing up.

"How are you, Bill?" said Whistler, stepping from his bedroom doorway.

"I hope you slept well, Bill," said Phly, sitting down on one of the chairs.

Both the alien and the elph were dressed in silver smocks, and like Tallulah, were smiling benevolently at him, their voices gentle.

"Um... I'm fine," said Bill, taking a step back and pressing himself against the wall. He suddenly felt terribly nervous.

The three of them went on looking at him with serene smiles. The antelope, meanwhile, had woken up, and was standing in the middle of the room with its ears pricked up, blinking repeatedly.

"What's that you've got there, Bill?" said Tallulah, in the same smooth, soft voice, gesturing towards his hand.

Bill opened his clenched palm, and showed her the wasp, still whirring in his hand. For a second, a dark look flickered across her eyes, but when she looked up, she was gently smiling at him again.

"That's nice, Bill," she said.

"Nice," chorused Whistler and Phly, both nodding slowly.

Bill blinked at the three of them. He would have expected Whistler to whip out the Knowletron to scan a strange new creature. Phly should be dashing forward to smother it in over-excited hugs, and Tallulah usually just rolled her eyes at anything the other two thought was interesting.

Bill dropped the wasp on the floor, and cleared his throat. "I think I might go for a walk," he said.

The three smiling faces all slowly shook their heads.

"I'm sorry, Bill," said Tallulah. "I'm afraid you can't do that."

"I can't?" stuttered Bill.

All three shook their heads again.

"We'd like you to stay here, Bill," said Whistler. "Don't you like it here?"

"I like it here, Bill. It's nice," said Phly. "Don't you think it's nice?"

"Yes," mumbled Bill, nodding quickly. "It's very nice. It's lovely."

"Then that's settled, Bill," said Tallulah, reaching out to take his hand in hers. "Why don't you come and sit with us, and we can have a little talk about how nice it is."

Bill tugged his hand away, and jumped as again the dark, angry look flickered across the blue eyes, then vanished. "I... er... didn't sleep all that well, actually," he said, sliding himself stiffly along the wall away from her. "I think maybe I'll just go and... have a little nap."

"That's a good idea, Bill," said Tallulah.

"There are visitors coming to see you later, Bill," said Whistler.

"It would be best if you're well rested, Bill," said Phly.

Bill swallowed hard, and took a hasty step towards the nearest bedroom, tangling his foot in his long smock. As he tumbled to the floor, he landed right in front of the liquid door of the chamber, which cascaded dutifully to the ground. At the end of the long, dimly lit silver corridor, hanging in the air like a small black cloud, was a swarm of metallic wasps.

"Follow," murmured the wasps, buzzing softly.

Bill struggled to his feet, and saw that Tallulah, Whistler and Phly were all slowly moving towards him, their arms outstretched. The smiles had been wiped from their faces, and now they simply stared at him intensely, as if they were very hungry and he was a piece of toast.

Bill flung himself into the corridor as quickly as he could, hitching up the skirts of the smock and hoping fervently he wouldn't trip again. He turned, and saw the watery door rise up from the silver floor, blocking his friends from his view.

Spinning round, he began to run down the silver corridor, hoping the swarming wasps would guide him to somewhere safe, since he had no idea where he was going. But as the next door cascaded to the floor, the wasps began to swarm about his head, and he realized to his horror that they would not lead him to safety.

"Follow," they buzzed in unison, like a train full of people wearing walkmans all playing the same tune. "Follow the Great Spondozo, he is your master."

The wasps flocked around his head, darting into his face, knotting themselves in his hair. He ducked and twirled and shook himself, flapping his hands and batting the tiny insects away, but they kept coming back, dive-bombing his face and scratching at his eyes with their metal legs. They were going for his nose again, he realized, trying to crawl up there like the one he'd sneezed out. He pinched his nose closed with two fingers, but then they began swarming around his open mouth, trying to crawl their way past his teeth. Bill clamped his lips shut, and tried to hold his breath, but they were still attacking his head, scoring his scalp with their tiny metallic feet, and buzzing madly in his ears.

My ears, thought Bill, and suddenly remembered the arena. Every creature in that room had worn those tubular steel headphones, and it wasn't until he'd taken the pair off that had so precariously balanced on top of his springy hair that he'd seen the first of the metallic wasps. The headphones weren't just for translation, he realized with a chill. They were there to make sure every single person at the conference had a wasp crawling around inside their head, without even knowing it was in there.

Every single person but Bill, with his overlong curls getting in the way.

If Bill had had time to stop and think, he would have made a mental note to thank his mother for agreeing never to take him back to the hairdresser. He would also have had time to be relieved that, instead of hating him, his friends were simply possessed by the tiny flying minions of an evil genius. Unfortunately, at that precise moment, those same friends were coming through the liquid door of their chamber, with their arms still reaching out towards him, and there wasn't time to do anything but run away.

Bill pelted away down the corridor, feeling the silver smock wrapping itself around his ankles and threatening to trip him with every step. His scarf flapped in his face; his sleeves fell down over his hands, and got in the way of him freeing his legs from his skirts. The wasps kept on buzzing around his face. And behind him the princess, the alien and the elph kept on coming, murmuring over and over, "Follow the Great Spondozo," as if they too had a part in a school play and needed to remember their lines.

The next door sploshed out of his way, and he ran on, through door after door, leaping clumsily over one before it had finished cascading, and finding himself barrelling head over heels into the next before it had even begun to liquefy. He picked himself up and kept going, still swatting at the wasps with a flapping sleeve, and noticing gratefully that the tail of his scarf had wrapped itself over his mouth and nose, letting him breathe without letting any of the wasps in. He hardly dared to glance over his shoulder: the droning hum of "Follow the Great Spondozo" followed at his heels close enough to tell him they were gaining on him.

As Bill ran through the nineteenth door, he breathed in sharply. The corridor had come to an end, and he was back out in the vast, cavernous room that held the arena. And while last time the silver walkway had slowly unfurled itself before them, flowing ahead with their every step, this time he wasn't walking. He ran out into thin air, before the flowing silver had time to keep up, and found himself standing on nothing at all.

Bill began to fall. He felt his hair lift off his face, but his ears were safe: he was tumbling faster than the wasps could fly, spinning over and over, the silver smock flying up over his head and blinding him.

He flailed his arms wildly, pulling the scratchy material off his face, and looking down, trying to see the floor.

There wasn't one. Only dim, bluish light, that glowed up at him from a fathomless depth. Bill looked up, and saw a similarly empty view. No floor. No sky. Nothing but falling, for ever and ever.

Bill gulped, and then realized he wasn't falling any more. A thin ribbon of silver had shot across the nothingness to cut off his descent, intercepting him so perfectly that his feet touched it with barely a jolt. He took a deep breath to steady himself, and then gasped. Striding down the silver walkway towards him was an endless stream of aliens, all wearing silver smocks and holding out their arms towards him. Even from this distance he could see their lips moving together, and hear the murmured words in the still air: "Follow the Great Spondozo, he is your master."

Bill began to run again, hearing the soft buzzing of another swarm of metallic wasps following him. The silver path stretched ahead of him, curving through the gloom, and he kept on running, not thinking of the stitch in his side, or the terrifying drop on either side of the walkway, or the glassy-eyed army behind him, but only of putting one foot in front of the other.

The silver path was twisting slowly towards another of the huge cylinders that seemed to rise from the dim glow below, and he followed it to an opening, finding himself inside again. Unlike the place he had slept in, this cylinder was hollow, and the walkway extended to the opposite side across a huge tube of space that was criss-crossed by countless more silver paths, above and below. All the way around the inner walls ran narrow circular platforms like vast flat doughnuts, one above the other, with doorways leading off them to other silver corridors.

Bill halted, peering down and seeing only more and more platforms stretching off into the distance below him. When he looked up, he could see people emerging from the doorways on the other side of the doughnut he was on, all dressed in silver, all chanting, "Follow the Great Spondozo," and all heading towards him.

Behind him, a hand brushed the back of his head, and he whirled to see a wrinkled Quxynggrotly at the head of the silver army, reaching out to grab him. With a yelp, Bill toppled backwards, falling off the platform.

His fall was broken almost at once by another of the silver walkways. He stumbled on his smock as he got up, slipping down another level and landing again on a silvery path cutting across the space between the platforms. It was a little like falling down stairs, which Bill was quite used to, except that usually when he got to the bottom he didn't have to deal with an army of alien zombies.

Scrambling to his feet, he ran along the walkway onto one of the platforms encircling the inside of the tube. While he was well-practised at falling, he was starting to feel thoroughly sore and even more out of breath, and knew he couldn't keep running for much longer. He spotted a silvery door in the cylinder wall, much larger and squarer than the rest, with the word 'EXIT' written beside it in enormous green neon letters. Scurrying towards it, he heard the swoosh of doors on the other side of the cylinder, announcing the arrival of more of the silver-smocked army.

As he got to the EXIT door, it began slowly to melt as the others had, merging with the silvery floor. But it wasn't a way out. The door opened onto nothingness.

"Where are you going, Bill?" said a soft voice behind him.

Bill turned, to see Tallulah, Whistler and Phly on the other side of the cylinder. Behind them was a vast crowd of bizarre creatures, all dressed in silver smocks.

"There's no point in running, Bill," said Whistler.

"You can't get away, Bill," said Phly.

Bill bit his lip, peering out of the EXIT and wondering if he should risk jumping out into thin air in the hope that a walkway would appear beneath him.

"That's not going to work, Bill," said Tallulah, as if reading his mind.

Bill turned back to look at her, and before his eyes every single silver walkway that connected the platforms above and below melted away. He shuffled tentatively towards the edge of the platform, and looked down. Nothing would break his fall if he slipped now.

"It's too late, Bill," said Phly.

The smocked figures began to fan out along the circular platform towards him, drawing closer and closer. Bill looked around desperately. There was an impossible drop before him; another behind.

There was no way out.

As Bill felt grasping hands reaching for his clothes, he lunged out with a shaking hand, and grabbed hold of the only weapon to hand: the neon EXIT sign. Clutching the letter I, he ripped it from the wall, sending a shower of sparks into the air. He held the green tube of light out in front of him like a sword, swooping it through the air. The silver-smocked army stepped back, alarmed.

The tube of light hummed in his hand, and for a moment Bill felt strangely powerful, as if there were an unknown force urging him on.

Then the I fizzed, sent up another shower of sparks, and went out. Bill stopped feeling all-powerful, and started feeling like a boy holding a warm tube of plastic.

The army took another step forwards, and Bill flung the I away, grabbing the X and swinging it in an arc towards Whistler. Again, a shower of sparks rained over the platform, and the army drew back with an anxious murmur, before the green glow fizzled and went out.

Bill grabbed the E, but it snapped the moment he lifted it up. The T lasted a little longer, but not long enough. The light died inside the clear tube, and Bill dropped it at his feet with a clatter.

Tallulah's blue eyes stared at him lifelessly. Phly's fuzzy arms reached up to grasp the tail of his scarf. The army pressed closer, filling the platform and threatening to spill out over the edge.

"I'm on fire!" said a familiar voice, loudly, and Bill turned to see Whistler smouldering next to the wall where the neon sign had been. Sparks still cascaded from the exposed wiring, and had dropped onto the smocks of several of the zombie-like aliens, igniting them immediately. The army seemed to have no idea what to do, and simply stood there, while their clothes were engulfed in small flames.

"Take them off!" shouted Bill urgently, realising the fire was spreading through the ranks of closely-packed beings. It wasn't their fault they were hunting him down, and even if it had been, being wrapped in foil and set alight seemed to Bill a pretty harsh punishment.

"Take them off," murmured the aliens, looking at one another in confusion.

"Yes, your clothes! Take them off!" yelled Bill, pulling the smock clumsily over his own head to demonstrate.

"Ahhhhhhh!" said the crowd, as one, and began fumbling and tugging at the scratchy cloth. Burning smocks rained down from the platform, dropping into the endless chasm below.

Bill gulped, as the grasping hands stopped tugging at their own clothes and started reaching after his again. He gazed desperately into the eyes of his friends, hoping that there might be a tiny scrap of them left that would take pity on him, but they stared back unseeingly. Bill closed his eyes, not wanting to look at their blank faces any more.

Then there was a loud pinging noise, and Bill found himself in an unexpected rainstorm.

He opened his eyes, and saw showers of water spraying every point in the room from tiny hoses in the base of each platform. The water soaked them instantly, dampening the last of the smouldering smocks.

"Sprinkler system activated," said a gentle, automated voice like the one in the Mercuroid. "Please proceed to your nearest fire exit and await further instructions."

All around him, the grasping hands paused in the air, and vacant-eyed beings stared upwards, blinking in the spray.

A shower of sparks to Bill's right made him jump sideways, thinking the EXIT sign's trailing wiring was about to blow up, but the sparks weren't coming from the wall. Flashes of light were spitting and darting out of Whistler's ear, crackling like a staticky TV. Whistler howled and moaned, putting his bony hands to his head, and then pulling them away as they were scorched by the flickering sparks.

Bill drew back, alarmed, but Tallulah and Phly were also covering their ears, their faces screwed up in pain, as sparks fizzed from the sides of their heads. All around the platform, the alien army was doubled over in agony.

The air grew warm, as the fine spray of water hissed and turned to steam. Then Bill realized that the rain falling down the chasm before him was not merely water: mingled in with the drips were tiny, smouldering lumps of metal.

As he watched, a charred, melted lump fell from Tallulah's ear. She blinked a few times, then pulled the wet hair that was plastered to her head out of her eyes, and prodded her ear with a finger as if it had just popped. She looked at Bill, and her blue eyes filled up with worry and guilt.

"*Pilf*, Bill," she said, in a faint voice. "We nearly…" She trailed off, staring round at the gathered crowd, and then looked down at the charred remains of her smock on the floor. Her nose wrinkled up into a familiar expression of disgust. "Ew, what was I *wearing*?" she spluttered.

Bill smiled, then fell backwards as something small, green, and bedraggled leapt into his arms.

"I'm so sorry!" squealed Phly, clinging to him with wet arms covered in spiky fuzz sticking up from the electric charges. "They told us to do bad things, and… ooh, clever Bill, making the wasps get all wet!"

"Bill, I don't know what to say," said a deep, emotional voice from above. Whistler held out a hand and pulled Bill back to his feet, the elph still wrapped around his neck. "No apology could ever be adequate," he went on, putting his shoulders back and talking to a point somewhere over Bill's head as if he were speaking to a large audience. "Our debt to you is greater than words can encompass… you have achieved something quite unspeakably remarkable here today…"

The crowd of assorted aliens murmured their agreement, nodding vigorously.

"Spare us the group hug, Whistle-boy," said Tallulah, giving Bill a nudge along the platform. "Let's get out of here."

As she spoke, an alarm began to sound, a high-pitched, wailing noise that rattled the floor.

"Ooh, what does that mean?" sang Phly, brightly, looking around to see where the sound was coming from.

"That's a warning siren," Whistler said, his grey face turning even greyer, as an anxious whispering broke out among the crowd. "A Gatherer patrol has just entered Quxyng space."

Chapter Eleven

The River

*… in which Phly goes home,
in a manner of speaking*

"Gatherers?" said Bill. "Here? Now?"

He felt Phly's grip around his neck tighten, as the crowd of aliens began shuffling and pushing on the narrow platform.

"Maybe the big noise went off by mistake," she sang, over the wail of the alarm.

As she spoke, Bill saw the yellow-dungareed Quxynggrotly who had guided them to the banquet battling through the throng to the cylinder wall. She swiped a wrinkled hand across its surface, and with a ripple a circle of light appeared. At first he thought it must be a window, but the image in the circle kept changing. The conference arena. The corridors outside the delegates' rooms. Deserted landing platforms.

A black, bulky spaceship, lowering its landing gear.

"Pilf," breathed Tallulah.

The ship was huge, a squarish mass with bulgy lumps

protruding from its sides. Black smoke belched from beneath. The booming sound as it touched down echoed so loudly, it sent ripples across the viewscreen.

"It doesn't look that big," said Bill, trying to sound like it was true.

"That's just a scout vessel," said Whistler. "There'll be more – " He broke off, whistling faintly as he gazed at the viewscreen.

Moving slowly towards the landing platforms, Bill could see three more ships. No, five. Maybe seven? He lost count, as the circular screen filled with black.

Panic broke out. The heaving crowd of aliens surged back towards the door on the opposite side of the platform, almost drowning out the warning siren with their shouting and whistling. Bill struggled to keep his feet, keeping tight hold of Phly as a terrified creature covered in blue feathers knocked into them, squawking wildly.

"What are we going to do?" Phly sang, in a shivery voice.

"The popular choice seems to be running," shouted Tallulah, pressing her back against the cylinder wall.

"Evidently," Whistler shouted back. "But where?"

The crowd had thinned out a little, but there was still a mob of panicky aliens struggling to get through the main door out of the cylinder. Bill peered over the edge of the platform, but there was nothing but a fathomless drop. He glanced up at the round viewscreen. The bulky black ships had all landed. He could see a mechanical ramp descending from the front of the nearest, belching more black smoke. Booted feet began to appear.

"Over here! Hurry!"

The wrinkled alien in the yellow dungarees was kneeling below the viewscreen, her bony fingers tracing a square on the silver wall. A curved panel of silver metal fell forward onto the platform with a clang, revealing a tunnel.

"Maintenance shaft?" Whistler shouted.

The alien woman nodded. "I don't know where it comes out, but it might buy you some time."

She turned to leave, but Phly scurried to her side and tugged on the leg of her dungarees. "Aren't you coming with us?" she chimed.

The Quxynggrotly smiled. "Oh, I'll be safer here. Don't worry, we have plenty of hiding places. Right now, I think you'd better get *him* as far away from here as possible."

She nodded her wrinkly head at Bill, then joined the crowd struggling through the main door. Bill stared after her, confused, but before he could ask what she meant, Tallulah gave him a shove, and he found himself slithering head-first down a sharply sloping slide, in total darkness. The shaft twisted around on itself a few times like a helter-skelter, then spat him out abruptly onto the hard floor of yet another silver corridor. Unlike the others, the walls and floor looked grimy and unpolished, and the lights kept flickering on and off.

Bill scrambled to his feet, just in time to avoid Phly, who hurtled out of the shaft so fast she crashed into the opposite wall. Whistler and Tallulah followed moments later.

"Now *that's* how to travel," said Tallulah, grinning as

she dusted off her hands. She wrinkled up her nose. "Pilf, Whistler. I can see why you showed us the upstairs first. This makes my place look clean."

"I'm all mucky!" sang Phly, holding out her robes and showing off the black smudges.

Whistler coughed. "It's known as the Under Zone," he said, waving a dismissive hand. "Obviously, someone like myself doesn't spend a great deal of time down here."

"Is that your way of saying we're lost?" said Tallulah.

"Of course not. Our best course would be to go…"

Bill frowned. Phly's cloak had begun to chime, the fringes faintly tinkling in a quick, repeated rhythm like a heartbeat.

The sound was faint, but definitely there. Heavy footsteps, thrumming through the floor. Getting closer.

"Away from that noise?" suggested Tallulah, sprinting off in the other direction.

Bill ran after her, feeling his feet protesting at every step. They followed the curve of the corridor to a junction, where the path forked. Whistler hesitated, and with a scowl Tallulah charged down the right tunnel, where the lights were dimmest. At the next junction, she swung off to the left, down a corridor littered with pieces of junk, then took another sharp right. Phly kept falling behind, and her cloak was making so much noise that Whistler scooped her up, and loped along behind them with her softly jingling in his arms.

Bill kept up with the princess as best he could, but whichever way they turned, the marching footsteps seemed to be gaining on them. As they staggered around another corner, Tallulah skidded to a halt.

"Dead end!" she yelled, turning on her heel and heading back the way she'd come, but Whistler slumped against the wall that blocked their escape.

"This is hopeless," he panted, dropping Phly to the floor. "We can't outrun them."

"What do you propose, a frontal assault?" snapped Tallulah, breathing hard. "I've got nothing against a good scrap, but we're a little bit on the weaponless side. Bill, any ideas?"

Bill stared at her, too exhausted even to laugh at the thought. He wiped sweat out of his eyes and listened, picking out the thumping of boots over his own noisy breathing. They were even closer now. But above them he could make out something else: a determined, repetitive 'eef'ing, somewhere not all that far away.

"The antelope," he murmured, trying to trace the source of the sound. Then he heard it again, even clearer.

"*Eef!*"

"This wall," said Bill, stepping past the alien to the wall that blocked the corridor. "It's behind this wall!"

"Great, Bill, just great," said Tallulah, peering back down the dim corridor. Dark figures could be seen approaching in the flickering yellow light. "Can we figure out a way to rescue the antelope *after* we figure out a way to rescue ourselves?"

"That's no wall," said Whistler, suddenly. "That's a *door*. The Under Zone is a little primitive, I'm afraid." He pressed a hand against it. The silver surface rippled, but instead of cascading into the floor, the liquid metal solidified into a door handle under Whistler's palm. He gave it a swift turn, and flung the door open.

The dim corridor stretched on into the distance, but standing in a shaft of light less than 20 metres away was the antelope.

"Eef," it said, performing an anxious tap-dance.

"Hello, lovely antelope!" sang Phly, springing forwards, then stopping with a squeak, and turning back towards them.

"Ow!" yelled Tallulah, as they collided. "Go that way, you flinker! There's a pilfing great squad of… Oh, no."

Emerging from the darkness beyond the antelope was another squad of Gatherers. They marched towards him, two by two, their pounding boots making the floor vibrate. He could smell oil and grease on the air, and there was the creak of flexing leather. Bill spun about, and saw the same image coming up the corridor behind them, only these were even closer. They looked like men, huge men in uniforms of battered black leather, smeared and filthy. Only they had no faces, just a smooth blank curve where their eyes should be.

"Eef!" said the antelope again, tap-dancing with more urgency. Bill tore his eyes from the approaching Gatherers. Beneath the antelope's hooves was a shiny, polished silver disc.

"Is that…?" said Bill.

"A Mercuroid!" Whistler finished for him.

"Nice one, 'lopey!" yelled Tallulah, hurling herself forwards.

Bill stumbled after her, trying to focus on the Gatherers he was running away from, and ignore the ones he was running towards. As their feet touched the circle, the silver began to shimmer. The liquid walls of the egg rose up, blocking out the echoing footsteps of the Gatherers, and sealing them safely inside. The engines fired with an enormous bang, and the Mercuroid shot out into space.

Bill sank to the curving floor of the egg. Every bit of him ached from running. He was quite accustomed to being pursued by disaster, but even for him this seemed to be getting out of hand.

"He had us!" Tallulah said, smacking her fist into her palm. "And then we did it! *Again*! Got away right under their stinking Gatherer noses! That'll teach the Great Spondozo to mess with us. I'll stick a stupid talking wasp in his ear, and see how he likes it. Get him to wash his face, and make his hair all neat and disgusting, and wear a stupid shiny dress!"

She ran her dirty fingers through her hair, just to check it was properly tangled.

"And make him free all the slaves," piped up Phly from the floor.

"What?" said Tallulah crossly. "Oh, yeah. Them too. How's that Plan coming, Bill?"

"Plan?" said Bill. "We're still doing the Plan?"

"After what just happened, I don't see that we have a choice," said Whistler. "The Great Spondozo took over the minds of an entire planet to capture you, and you still got away. I don't imagine he's going to just forget about it, do you?"

Bill stared at the alien. "But the wasps were there to stop the peace conference," he said, haltingly. "That's why the Gatherers came."

"Maybe so," said Tallulah, "but that wasp in my head was pretty specific about keeping hold of you. It told us to..."

She paused. There was a sniff from the floor, and Bill turned to see Phly shuddering, her big dark eyes welling up with tears.

"Well, it doesn't matter what it said," muttered Tallulah, clearing her throat and giving the elph's little shoulder a squeeze. "But apparently the Great Spondozo's not exactly your biggest fan."

There was an uncomfortable silence, broken only by an anxious rumbling in Bill's stomach. When Owen Silva had sentenced him to death, he'd been fairly sure there had simply been a slight misunderstanding. Now, it was starting to look personal.

"Maybe you should do the Plan without me," he mumbled, looking at his shoes.

"Don't be such a flinker," said Tallulah, breaking into a grin. "That's what makes it so perfect. If he's after you anyway, we won't have to lift a finger. We can just sit back and wait for him to come and get you. And when he does – poom!"

"Poom?" said Bill.

"Yeah, poom!" said Tallulah, stumbling slightly as the Mercuroid juddered. "Hey, Whistler, where are we going, anyway?"

Whistler was frowning as he concentrated on the invisible controls, sending the egg into a series of small jerks. "Oh... nowhere in particular..." he said, with a faint whistle. "Just – er – drifting, really."

"We should find somewhere safe to lie in wait," said

Tallulah. "Somewhere the Great Spondozo hasn't taken over yet."

"Ooh, my home, my home!" squealed Phly, jumping up and down. "Can we, Whistler, please!"

A small smile crept across the alien's wrinkled face.

"Actually, Phly, that sounds like an excellent idea," he said, slipping his hand into the pocket of his dungarees and producing the Knowletron. He opened it, and began spinning through the globe of light. "I visited your layer some years ago. Quite remarkable flora."

Without warning, the antelope growled, rose to its hooves, and began butting Whistler in the knee with its pointy horns. Whistler ignored it, and swiped at the silver wall quickly. The antelope growled again, but Whistler closed the Knowletron with a snap.

"I've programmed the AND with new co-ordinates. It should be quite a short journey."

The antelope blinked at Whistler, then retreated, and curled up on the floor next to Phly. Whistler stared at the creature with a cold, yet slightly fearful expression, but when he realized Bill was watching him, he turned his face away.

Bill buried his nose in the warm wool of his scarf, and decided he was far too tired to argue. He wanted nothing more than to drift off into sleep, but every time he closed his eyes, he could see the blank faceless faces of the Gatherers, and hear the pounding rhythm of their heavy boots. He kept wondering what had happened to Trinkle and the others, and hoping it wasn't too awful, because it looked like sooner or later it might be happening to him.

The soft whine of the Mercuroid's engines changed their pitch, and Bill felt the floor tilting beneath him. Phly giggled as the egg rolled onto its side, and then onto its pointy end, tipping them all into a muddled tangle of arms, legs and small sharp horns.

"Please remain seated, your journey is almost completed," said a familiar soft voice.

"Sorry about this, crew," said Whistler, trying to sound dignified with a elph dangling around his neck and a large clumpy boot swinging dangerously close to his chin. He stretched out a thin grey arm, and swatted at a spot on the wall, triggering the porthole.

The silver wall rippled, and a circle appeared. Wherever they were, it looked very pink.

With a loud popping noise, the egg suddenly righted itself. It was still lurching oddly, but it was no longer quite so difficult to tell which way was up, and they could see sky through the porthole.

The Mercuroid was gently bobbing on a swift-flowing river, whose waters were bright pink and slightly creamy, like strawberry milkshake. The sky was a clear, sunny blue, and the river banks were lined with tall trees and vibrant flowers, all in full bloom.

"Auto-flotation," announced Whistler proudly, scanning their surroundings with the Knowletron. "Always takes a little while to kick in."

"Pink river," said Tallulah. "Now that's just... weird."

"I like pink," sang Phly softly, her eyes wide as if she was trying to make them big enough to take in all the colours.

From outside came a strange twanging noise. Then

Bill heard voices, what sounded like hundreds of voices, all singing together, though unfortunately not all singing quite the same tune. As they grew louder, he began to make out the words of the song:

> *O mighty egg, dropped from the sky,*
> *Have you ever wondered why*
> *The water's wet but grass is not?*
> *We contemplate such things a lot.*

Bill stared out of the porthole, but he could see nothing but the flowing river and the trees waving gently in the breeze as they floated along. Then the odd twanging began again, and the voices resumed their unmusical song:

> *O shiny egg, with silver sides,*
> *What secrets do your insides hide?*
> *It's like a star has tumbled down,*
> *Let's hope it knows how not to drown.*

"Where's it coming from?" said Tallulah, pressing her nose up close to the window and sending ripples across its surface.

Phly gave a tinkly giggle, and swished her robe in time with the rhythmic twanging. "Look," she sang, pointing a finger at the frothy pink water.

Outside, bobbing alongside the egg, were three enormous water lily leaves. Sitting on each one, holding a large leaf-shaped oar and paddling to keep up, were three small, fuzzy green people who looked remarkably familiar.

"Elphs," trilled Phly, hopping on one leg excitedly.

"Oh, joy," said Tallulah, rolling her eyes. "'Cause one just isn't enough."

The singing began again, this time accompanied by Phly humming happily along:

> *O happy egg, we're here to guide you,*
> *If you'll let us, we'll provide you*
> *Songs and gifts and lots of dancing,*
> *We think you'll find it quite entrancing.*

Tallulah groaned, but Bill thought that so long as he could opt out of the dancing, that didn't sound too bad. It was certainly a warmer welcome than Whistler's home had offered.

The three elphs steered the bobbing egg gently towards a wooden landing platform jutting out across the water. As the egg's silver side nudged gently against it, Whistler touched an invisible control, and the Mercuroid's silver walls began to melt away around them. The passengers hopped quickly onto the platform, Bill dipping only a metre or so of trailing scarf in the pink waters in the process. He gazed at the leafy river-bank in amazement, letting the sun warm his face, gulping in deep breaths of the cool, lightly perfumed air, and realising he was smiling broadly for the first time in what seemed like days.

Now they were up close, Bill found it was easy to tell the other elphs apart from Phly. All three were slightly taller, and their green fuzz was a shade paler than hers. The tallest wore a flowing robe like Phly's, except that it had a network of sparkling threads woven through the fabric, as if she had just run through a curtain of dewy spiders' webs. The next had violets growing from two large pockets full of earth in the front of her robe, which rose to form a wreath about her squirrelish ears. Last, and shortest, was a squat, pot-bellied elph with a luxurious curly green beard that reached almost to his fuzzy toes.

The three elphs had steered their lily boats up to the platform, and leapt enthusiastically towards the strangers, jingling and humming and clapping their hands. Phly instantly joined in, and the four of them started whirling around, hand in hand, their robes chiming and their many voices laughing notes high and low. Like the singing, the whirling was rather haphazard, and Bill was almost knocked into the river several times, but it was hard not to smile at the sight (unless, of course, you were Tallulah, who was yawning and pointedly looking bored).

Whistler too seemed to think the dancing had gone on long enough, and cleared his throat.

"Perhaps some introductions might be in order," he said, drawing his shoulders back and puffing out his chest. "My name is…"

Before he could launch into his numerous names, the elphs formed a line and swept into a deep bow.

The elph with the sparkly robe stood up.

"Phlippa," she sang, loudly.

The elph with the crown of violets lifted her head.

"Phenella," she chanted, swishing her cloak.

The squat elph with the beard stood up straight.

"Phrank," he bellowed.

Then he grabbed a fistful of his beard, pulled the strands of curly green hair out straight in front of his chin, and began plucking them like the strings of a banjo.

A familiar twanging filled the air, and the three elphs sang together:

> *Phenella, Phlippa, beardy Phrank,*
> *We live on the river-bank,*
> *We love birds and trees and flowers,*
> *We can sing like this for hours.*

"Aren't we the lucky ones," grumbled Tallulah.

The elphs bowed and smiled, clapping themselves cheerfully. Then they looked expectantly at the new arrivals.

Bill stopped smiling, and began to feel rather nervous, but Phly jumped forwards at once, her big eyes shiny with bashful excitement as she sang:

> *I am Phly, Phly am I,*
> *Lately fallen from the sky!*
> *I like the way your river's pink,*
> *I'm going to like it here, I think.*

Again, the elphs applauded, hopping up and down. Then they went quiet again, and looked at Bill, Tallulah, Whistler and the antelope in eager anticipation. Bill felt the nervous feeling get worse, and he frantically tried to think up words that rhymed with 'Bill'. There were quite a few, but none of them seemed to fit together to make a song.

Beside him, Whistler seemed to be having the same problem. He was smoothing a bony hand over his wrinkly forehead, whistling faintly. Assuming this was a musical introduction, Phly, Phlippa, Phenella and Phrank gathered at his feet.

"Ahem," said Whistler, in an unusually quavery voice. "My name... er..."

Wiping his hand over his head, he started again. "I am a Quxynggrotly."

There was a long, whistly pause.

"And I have travelled... a lot-ly," he added, faltering as Tallulah snorted behind him.

Phly clapped wildly. The other elphs broke out into warm smiles and clapped too, before all four enveloped Whistler's legs in a tangled, chiming hug. Whistler smiled, obviously pleased.

"Thank you, thank you," he said, airily waving a hand.

"It was lovely," sang Phly cheerily, releasing Whistler's leg and bounding over to stand in front of Bill.

Bill gulped, as the other elphs joined her.

"Um," he said, his mouth feeling unpleasantly dry. "My name is Bill."

The four small green faces went on staring up at him expectantly.

"I feel quite ill," he said.

Still the big wide eyes looked up.

"No, really, I do," he said quickly, as his stomach grumbled. "Is that enough?"

The elphs looked at one another, nodding slowly and humming to themselves, before breaking out into a flurry of applause.

"*Specially* good," said Phenella.

"Most unusual," said Phlippa.

"Very modern," said Phrank, patting Bill's leg encouragingly.

Bill blushed, feeling relieved. He caught Whistler

looking at him rather sourly through the corner of his eye, as the elphs moved on to Tallulah, who had flopped down under the nearest tree and was leaning back against the trunk with her eyes closed. Before the elphs could get too close, she held up a warning hand.

"Forget it, tinkletoes," she said, still with her eyes shut. "No singing. No poetry. I'd rather snog the Great Spondozo."

The four elphs put their heads close together, and hummed and whispered to one another. Then they straightened up, and smiled proudly.

"Since Tallulah doesn't want to sing her own song, we're going to sing one for her," announced Phly.

Tallulah opened one blue eye, and gave Phly a stern look.

"It's called 'O the green mountains of my homeland, how very pointy are they'," Phlippa added, solemnly.

"Wait," said Bill, as he watched Tallulah's look change from stern to fierce. "What about the antelope?"

"Excellent point, Bill," added Whistler swiftly. "Best finish the introductions, eh?"

The antelope trotted forward and blinked.

"Hello, 'lope!" sang Phly, giving it a friendly pat on the head. "Will you sing us a song too?"

Tallulah's murderous expression gave way to her usual scornfully wrinkled nose. But before she could say anything rude, Phlippa, Phenella and Phrank chorused together:

> *Songs worthy of this antelope*
> *Shall come to us in time, we hope.*

As they sang, Phrank played an especially twangy and complicated accompaniment on his beard. The antelope blinked repeatedly, as if to say thank you.

A high, fluting sound rang through the air, and a large bird with strikingly unlikely red, purple and orange feathers swooped down low over their heads.

"Ooh!" squeaked Phly, as the bird circled above them. "Is that who I think it is?"

The three other elphs nodded so vigorously, their earrings almost drowned out the piping of the bird's song.

"The Dinner Bird!" they sang together.

The bird circled in the air once more, then swooped back into the trees and out of sight.

"Hope you're hungry!" sang Phenella, seizing Bill's hand, and tugging him into the forest.

It was not like any wood he'd ever been in. The trees and flowers seemed to have politely chosen to grow in neat, ordered rows, leaving a broad winding path for them to walk down. There were no dead leaves on the ground, no broken twigs or wilting blooms. Even the mud beneath his feet smelled oddly clean. Bill noticed Phly sniffing the air, looking slightly puzzled, but Whistler was tapping away at the Knowletron, ignoring all Phlippa's attempts to hurry him along, and Tallulah was clearly enjoying pulling faces at the small, flop-eared rabbits that kept hopping into her path. Phenella, meanwhile, was so determined to catch up with the Dinner Bird that by the time they reached the end of the path, Bill was quite breathless.

The moment he entered the elphs' camp, however, all traces of weariness melted away. They had emerged into a wide clearing, perfectly round, carpeted with young green grass. Around the edges of the circle, in the shade of the trees, were woven baskets piled high with brightly-coloured fruits. In the centre a fire blazed, sending sweet-smelling wood smoke spiralling upwards. A cooking pot hung over the fire, and neat parcels wrapped in leaves rested on the stones around its edge. The sun beat down warmly, but a gentle breeze fanned his face. It was extraordinarily peaceful.

The Dinner Bird flew once round the clearing, then disappeared back into the forest, still singing.

"Thank you, Dinner Bird!" chorused the elphs, waving as they skipped over to the fire.

Laid out on the ground were wooden bowls, and Phly and Phrank began ladling out thick soup from the cooking pot. Phlippa and Phenella disappeared into the trees, and emerged again a moment later with small bundles of cloth under their arms. Bill expected them to roll them out on the ground like a patchwork picnic blanket, but instead the elphs strung them up around the edge of the clearing, and soon there were eight small hammocks swinging low to the ground. They looked like the sort of thing his granny might have dreamed up for the family barbecue at the Sunnyglades retirement home, just to make sure there would be lots of other people's grannies there too, to watch Bill topple to the ground.

"Go on, it's ever so comfy," sang Phenella, giving him an encouraging push.

He did, of course, fall out, but only three times, which was only one more than Tallulah, and considerably fewer than Whistler, who was far larger than the hammock and in the end had to lie across it sideways, with his head and legs dangling over the sides. The elphs decided falling out was an excellent new game, and had a giggly time copying them, until Phrank managed to get his beard tangled in the knotty cloth and ended up hanging by it, kicking his little feet helplessly, at which point they decided food was more fun.

Although it was rather difficult to eat soup lying in a hammock, the food was so delicious that Bill quickly forgot such worries. With the hot soup there were thick slices of a sweet, cake-like bread for dunking; after the soup, the parcels from the fire circle were unwrapped to reveal what looked like baked potatoes, except they were dark orange and had butter and melted cheese already on the inside. The elphs then raided the fruit baskets under the trees, and the one that looked like a very small blue banana quickly became Bill's favourite, once he'd discovered it was the skin that was nice and the squashy bit in the middle that you threw away. All of it was washed down with a purple bubbly drink that the elphs squeezed from fruits which made a loud popping noise when they were crushed.

"Wonderful, simply wonderful," said Whistler, his eyes glazing over as he finished a juicy green peach, and groped for another. "I really must take some readings." He took a little bite, and sighed with pleasure. "Later. *Much* later."

The three elphs skipped between the hammocks,

bringing bowl after bowl of strange and enticing food. Tallulah was making small happy groaning noises as she chewed on the petals of a white flower, dipped in the purple pop juice. The antelope was gnawing leaves off the trees, 'eef'ing contentedly. Only Phly seemed to be lacking in appetite, and sat clutching a single brown fruit, nibbling at it.

"No offence, Bill," said Tallulah, finally pausing between mouthfuls for long enough to speak, "but this is better than bacon sandwiches."

Bill popped a handful of sweet berries into his mouth, and found himself smiling in agreement. His aching legs and sore feet now felt lighter than air. When he closed his eyes, he could hear soft, tinkling laughter, and smell wood smoke mingling with lilac and lavender. Cool breezes played through his hair, as if loving hands were stroking his head. The clearing was growing darker, and he could just make out stars sparkling in the early dusk sky. Phrank began plucking at his beard-banjo, humming a low, soothing tune. A gentle snoring, punctuated by whistling, drifted through the clearing. Bill felt his eyes dropping closed. He could stay here forever, he thought, perfectly safe. The Great Spondozo couldn't bother him now. Nothing could possibly come to any harm surrounded by such tranquil beauty.

When he opened his eyes again, the clearing was lit only by the campfire. He sat up awkwardly, wondering what had woken him. By the flickering flames, he could see his friends slumbering peacefully in their hammocks…

One of the hammocks was empty.

Scrambling to his feet as quietly as possible, he crept across to the empty hammock. It was Phly's. Bill backed away, deciding to wake Tallulah and risk an earful, when a noise made him halt.

Someone was crying. Softly, musically, with a low chiming accompanying every shuddering breath.

He stared in the direction of the melancholy sound, and caught a glimpse of light in the trees. It flickered out of view for a moment, then reappeared, moving slowly away from the clearing. Bill hesitated, still wondering whether to wake the princess, but somehow he wasn't sure Tallulah would be much help. He wasn't sure he'd be much help either, but with a grimace, he stepped out of the clearing into the forest.

It was cooler under the trees, and Bill moved quickly, grateful there were no loose twigs or roots to trip him. He kept his arms outstretched, and tried to ignore the darkness, focusing on the flicker of light.

The sound of crying grew louder, and Bill realized the light had stopped moving. He ran the last few paces, and stepped out from the trees onto the edge of a cliff. The night sky was bright with stars, and he could clearly see stretched out far below a river running through a deep canyon, and beyond, the craggy tips of a range of mountains. On the ground, swinging her little feet off the edge of the cliff, was Phly. In her cupped palms was a small fire, hissing as large tears rolled down her squirrelish nose and plopped into the flames.

"Phly, what's wrong?" said Bill, dropping to his knees beside her, and keeping a wary eye on the edge of the cliff.

"Everything," she sang, in a wretched tone.

"But I thought you were happy to be home?"

"That's just it," she sniffed, the flames leaping in her huge, wet eyes. "I'm not home. And now I never will be."

Bill frowned, but she pointed at the rocky outline of peaks in the distance. "I'm a mountain elph, not a river elph. Over there, that's my real home."

"Well, that's all right," said Bill, smiling with relief. "We can go there in the morning."

Phly shook her head miserably. "No point," she sang. "It'll be wrong too. It was wild and free and beautiful, and now it will all be wrong. Oh, how can they not have noticed! Why can't they see how terrible it is?"

"But this place is fantastic!" said Bill. "All these plants, and the sunshine, and the food. It's… well, it's *perfect*."

Phly lifted her shiny eyes up to his. Bill stared at her mournful face, and his shoulders slumped forward. "And that's why it's wrong," he said, slowly.

The elph nodded. "The trees used to grow wherever they wanted. The grass would grow long, long till you got lost in it, and sometimes it rained. The flowers would bloom, and then they'd die, and there were thorns on the stems to prick you, and mud up to your knees sometimes – proper mud, that smells all dirty." She managed a sad little smile. "Maybe it wasn't as nice," she sang, "but it was real."

"But who would do something like that?" said Bill. "Who would come to your world and mess it all up…" He groaned as the realization hit him. "The Great Spondozo. He's already been here."

Phly nodded again. "I think so," she sniffed.

Bill hung his head. It had felt so wonderful to just let go for a few hours; to lie back, and laugh, and forget. But now, he'd have to face it all again. There was good reason to be afraid. And he was running out of places to hide.

"I'd better go and warn the others," he said wearily, standing up. "We'll probably have to start..."

He broke off, as a piercing scream rang out from the trees.

"Wake up, you idiots!" It was Tallulah, yelling at the top of her lungs. "Wake up! We're under attack!"

Chapter Twelve

The Council of the Wronged

... in which Bill meets some old friends,
and loses some new ones

"Oh, no," whispered Bill, staring into the dark forest, as Tallulah's voice echoed through the trees. "We're too late."

He turned to ask Phly what to do, but the elph had leapt up with a jingle, and was disappearing into the forest. He had a nagging suspicion that running *towards* the noise might not be the safest move, but now he was standing, alone, in almost total darkness. Taking a deep breath, he plunged into the trees after her.

The chimes of her cloak led him on down the path, but before long he could find his own way. The campfire in the clearing was blazing high in the air, clearly visible through the trees. He could hear shouting, a low whistling, and what sounded very much like laughter. Under it all was a strange creaking noise, and the earth beneath his feet seemed to rumble, as if something deep below was stirring.

Bill slowed down as he drew close to the edge of the forest, panting hard, and found Phly hiding behind a tree. He crouched down beside her and stared out into the clearing, steeling himself for what he might see.

Beside the fire was what appeared to be a pile of bodies. The pile was moving, and Bill realized the movement came not only from the struggling bodies, but from the thick ropes tying them down: they were green and leafy, and seemed to have emerged from the grassy floor of the clearing to twine themselves around their victims.

Standing with a boot resting on the pile, triumphantly dusting off her hands, was Tallulah.

"Oi, Phly, turns out your mates are pretty handy in a punch-up," she yelled, giving their hiding place a thumbs up. "If they could cut down on the poetry, I might even start to like them."

Bill stepped into the clearing, slightly embarrassed by their failure to hide, and found Whistler cowering under his hammock. Phly reluctantly followed him out, avoiding the three river elphs who were skipping joyfully round the fire.

"Bindervines," she sang softly, stroking the leafy ropes.

"Bindervines!" sang the river elphs.

"Whatever they are, they took out a Gatherer patrol faster than any cannon I've seen. Right, fellas?" Tallulah gave the wriggling heap of bodies a kick.

There was a metallic clang, and a muffled voice floated up from the pile.

"Do you mind? This armour's brand new!"

Bill frowned. The voice sounded oddly familiar. Cautiously, he stepped a little closer, and caught a glimpse of a rust-red breastplate gleaming in the firelight. Poking out from between the leafy coils he could also make out a lilac shin-guard, a shiny green gauntlet, and, right at the bottom, a polished grey shoe, which the antelope was sniffing suspiciously.

"I don't think that's a Gatherer patrol," Bill said, slowly.

"Gatherers? Us?" came another muffled voice from the heap. "How ridiculous!"

"Look, look," sang Phly, her eyes widening as she tugged a vine away. "It's the knights!"

"Hello!" said the rust-red knight, as his face appeared from under the green coils. "Princess Tallulah! Sir Bill!"

The green gauntlet flapped a feeble greeting.

"Ooh, Phly, did you bring us some more nice friends?" sang Phlippa, still skipping.

"Er... I don't suppose you could let us up?" said the rust-red knight, rather breathlessly. "I'm... a little bit... squashed..."

"Try being at the bottom," croaked a cold voice.

The three river elphs giggled, then began to hum, deep and low. The raging flames of the campfire died down, and Bill felt the ground under his feet rumbling again, as the bindervines began to loosen their grip on their captives. The leafy green coils slithered back into the earth, and moments later four familiar figures were lying on the grass.

The three knights had obviously gone through some kind of change in fortunes since Bill had last seen them.

The rust-red knight's breastplate was now rust-red on purpose; all three wore quite extraordinarily shiny armour, with not a dent or a scratch in sight. The lilac knight carried a sword with a hilt so encrusted with amethysts he could barely wrap his fingers around it; the green knight bore a shield emblazoned with a fire-breathing dragon, its scales studded with emeralds. Despite the weight of their armour, as they got to their feet Bill noticed all three seemed to stand a little taller than he remembered.

The same could not be said for their companion. Curled in a pathetic ball on the floor, his hands tied behind him with a tasselled golden cord, lay Owen Silva. His immaculate pinstriped suit was now filthy and torn, the manicured fingernails were black with dirt, and his silver hair fell in lank, greasy clumps over his eyes. He struggled to his knees, but a prod from Tallulah's boot sent him crashing back to the ground.

The river elphs looked doubtful, but Tallulah gave them a warning look. "Trust me, this one's not so nice," she said.

"Ahem!" said Whistler, finally emerging from under his hammock. He shook hands with the knights, keeping a wary distance from Silva. "Terribly sorry about all the confusion, Sir Knights. I'm afraid our elph friends are a little overzealous in protecting their camp."

"Unlike some people," murmured Tallulah.

"That's all right," said the rust-red knight.

"Good practice for us," said the lilac knight.

"Think we might need to work on our ambush technique," said the green knight, polishing a grassy stain off his armoured elbow.

"You needn't bother," came a smug voice from the floor. "When he hears what you've done to me, it'll take more than an overpriced new outfit to save you from the Great... Ow!"

Silva broke off with a howl, as the antelope sank its pointy teeth into his shoulder. In a moment, the knights were holding three long, shining blades to Silva's throat.

"I think the Great 'Ow' is the least of your worries, matey," grinned Tallulah, as the bank manager shrank away from the swords. "Now then. How about a little more of that elph hospitality?"

The three river elphs clapped their hands with delight, and dashed off to gather fruit from under the trees. But Bill looked at Phly, who was staring mournfully at the floor, swishing her cloak around her as if hoping the chimes would cheer her up.

"Wait," he said. "There's something you should know. Something *bad*."

All eyes turned to him. He faltered for a moment under Whistler's searching gaze, but Tallulah grabbed his arm and pulled him towards the fire.

"Shut it," she hissed, then grinned at the knights. "Grab a hammock, lads," she said, loudly. "And get some of that purple stuff down you, you're going to love it."

"No, wait," Bill protested, as the elphs pressed cups of purple juice into the knights' hands. "You don't understand, the Great-"

Tallulah brought her boot down hard on his foot, and silenced him with a glare.

"Yeah, we get it, the Great Spondozo's already been here," she whispered grimly, switching quickly to a smile as Phrank hopped over to collect a baked potato, then rolling her eyes at Bill's look of surprise. "I'm not a total halfwit, you know," she muttered. "This place seems great, but Phly's moping about like someone stole her favourite blade of grass, and she might be a pain, but she's one almighty weathervane. Something round here's just... *off*, know what I mean?"

Bill nodded. "That's why we need to tell the-"

Tallulah raised an eyebrow, and nodded at the knights. The rust-red knight and the lilac knight were lustily singing along with the elphs' latest song, 'Little Puffy Clouds are Nice', despite not knowing the words, while Phenella festooned the green knight with violets.

"Look at them," said the princess. "Those elphs haven't got a clue. Think they'd be happier if they knew?"

Bill looked at Phly's dismal face, and slowly shook his head. "So we shouldn't tell anyone? Just stay here, and hope no one notices?"

"You're joking," said Tallulah. "You saw what happened on Quxyng. Pilf knows why, but the Great Spondozo's after you, and he isn't going to stop hunting you down till he's got you. The longer we stay here, the more likely it is their happy little la-la land goes bye-bye. Besides, those knights are looking pretty handy. Let them get some food down them, and once the little green gang have nodded off, we'll fill them in. Then we can all leg it back to the egg, and get on with the Plan."

Taking Bill's silence for agreement, Tallulah slapped him on the back, fixed a big smile on her face, and grabbed a cup of purple pop juice. Bill swallowed, and sat down with the knights, who were trying to eat baked potatoes without getting butter on their pristine gauntlets. Silva was spitting out the berries Phlippa offered him, but the knights tucked in hungrily, much to the elphs' delight.

"Vital to keep one's strength up," said the rust-red knight, sinking his teeth into a fist-sized hunk of cake.

"A warrior never knows when he'll have time to eat again," said the lilac knight, licking his bowl clean.

The green knight lay back in a hammock, as a giggling Phenella dropped plump orange grapes into his mouth. Even Bill found himself nibbling anxiously on a few more blue banana skins. But eventually the happy sounds of munching and chewing subsided, and the party lapsed into contented silence.

Bill noticed Tallulah was fidgeting in her hammock, as if she could feel a sneeze coming on, but didn't quite want to let it go.

"So… er… how are things back home, anyway?" she said, clearly trying to sound casual. "Anything… you know… *important* that I ought to know about?"

"Oh, one or two little changes," said the lilac knight, chuckling.

The rust-red knight gave Bill a smile. "You made quite an impression, Sir Bill."

The green knight stroked his shield bashfully. Bill looked at the jewel-studded dragon again, and realized with a blush that it was being stabbed in the neck by a tiny, scarf-wearing figure.

"It didn't take too long to overpower the guards in the bank, once we'd remembered we were supposed to be really hurting them," the rust-red knight continued. "You know, proper fighting."

"With real blood and everything!" added the lilac knight.

There was a low hum from the river elphs, as if they didn't entirely approve.

"And once they were out of the way, there was only one thing left to do," said the rust-red knight.

"Lock up Owen Silva?" said Bill.

"No," said the lilac knight. "*Shopping*. No one was going to take us seriously in our old gear."

"I had a devil of a time choosing the colour: Minty Pasture, Ocean Jade…" said the green knight, admiring his armoured arm as the firelight bounced off it, "but I couldn't be happier with the finish."

"Oh, I know," said the lilac knight. "Apple Meadow is just so *you*."

Tallulah cleared her throat pointedly. "And *then* you got Owen Silva?"

The rust-red knight nodded. "Bit of a disappointment, that," he sighed. "We charged up there, all set to try out our new swords, and he was hiding under his desk with his fingers in his ears."

Silva made a spluttering noise, but the antelope was standing guard over him, and after a stern blinking Silva fell quiet.

"After that, things moved pretty quickly," the rust-red knight continued. "Once word got out that Silva wasn't running things any more, it was almost like he'd never been there. We did blow up a bit of the high street, just for old times' sake…"

Tallulah turned slightly pale.

"But we decided it wasn't really very becoming, now we were real knights," said the lilac knight. "So we had a big party instead. Plenty of bacon sandwiches."

"King Fernando sends his best, by the way, Tallulah," added the green knight. "He knew we'd catch up with you sooner or later."

Tallulah's face flushed pink, and she breathed out a long sigh of relief. Realising Bill was watching her, she shuffled her shoulders awkwardly. "Yeah, well, I knew the old man would be all right," she mumbled. Then she frowned. "How did he know you'd catch up?"

"An excellent question," said Whistler, regarding the knights with suspicion. "How exactly did you travel here?"

The rust-red knight smiled. "Everyone saw you escaping in the flying egg. It didn't take him over there long to let slip he had another one hidden at The Fox and Jockey."

"I always knew that Queen Enid was dodgy," muttered Tallulah.

"Of course, the moment we arrived we knew we'd be seeing you soon," the rust-red knight continued.

"There could hardly be a more likely place to find it," said the lilac knight.

"And once we did, we knew you couldn't be far behind," said the green knight. "It is Boyland's quest, after all."

Bill's eyes opened wide. "Quest?" he said.

"It was me that actually found it," the green knight blushed, as the other two gave him clanking pats on the back. "I've been keeping it safe ever since."

He popped open his shining breastplate. A soft leather pouch, like a money-bag, hung around his neck. He knelt down before Bill, and reverently held up the pouch. Bill hesitated, then took the bag, and gingerly opened it up. His fingers brushed against something slimy that moved, and with a yelp, he dropped it.

The green knight looked rather put out, and picked the pouch up, emptying it into his hand. A snail the size of a golf ball, with a bright golden shell, began to trail across his gleaming gauntlet.

"Behold, Sir Bill," he said, proudly. "The Holy Snail!"

Bill's mouth fell open, but before he could say a word, the night air was suddenly filled with a terrible wailing, as if hundreds of voices were crying out in anguish.

"Snail thieves!" shouted Phrank accusingly.

"Bad nice new friends!" howled Phlippa, stamping her foot.

"Oh, and bad elph, bad bad elph!" cried Phenella, pointing a fuzzy finger at Phly, whose dark eyes were filling with tears.

Bill felt the ground shudder. Then he was yanked from behind by the ankles, and dragged along the grass. He reached down, trying to free himself, but his wrists were seized and pulled up over his head. He looked up, and saw thick green vines coiling around his arms, snaking towards his throat. Then the world seemed to spin around him, and he found himself dangling upside down. He struggled, but the bindervines holding his legs in the air merely tightened their grip. Leafy tendrils wound themselves into his hair. Even his scarf, which was trailing down to the ground, was tightly bound in green coils, leaving only tufts of fluffy blue and scratchy pink visible.

He looked around dizzily. The three knights were bundled up together in a tight knot of green rope, their armour clanking and buckling under the strain. Whistler was pinned to the trunk of a tree; Tallulah had been trussed up in her hammock like a cocoon. Silva and the antelope were dangling from an overhanging branch, knotted together, neither one of them looking particularly happy about it. And Phly was lost somewhere in the middle of a huge ball of seething vines, high above the other three elphs.

Phlippa, Phenella and Phrank's dark eyes seemed to blaze in the firelight, and as they turned their gaze on him, Bill shivered.

"Now, I'm sure this all just a... a slight misunderstanding," said Whistler, his voice sounding faint.

Phlippa cast a look in his direction, and a tendril of bindervine snaked swiftly across Whistler's mouth.

"That bit about getting to like you?" shouted Tallulah, from inside her hammock. "I take it back!"

With one look from Phenella, she too was silenced.

Bill swallowed hard, as the three elphs moved to stand in a line before him. The vines holding him creaked and shifted, lowering him so his face was level with theirs, though still upside down.

"Oh, Bill," sang Phlippa, severely.

"We liked you," sang Phenella, shaking petals from her head.

"We thought you liked us," sang Phrank, twanging a low note from his beard.

"But I did!" said Bill, desperately. "I do!" He eyed the vines clutching at his hair warily, but they stayed away from his mouth. "Please, this is all just a mistake!"

"You sent them here," sang Phlippa, her voice sounding harsher.

"Men with swords," sang Phenella, stamping her foot.

"To steal a poor, defenceless creature!" sang Phrank, snapping the hairs of his beard in his fury.

"No, I didn't," Bill began, then hesitated. "Well, I sort of did… but I really didn't mean to." He tailed off. It sounded feeble, even to him.

"What happens now?" he asked in a tentative voice, not sure he wanted to know the answer.

"Now," sang Phlippa, "we summon the Council of the Wronged."

Phrank strummed a dismal chord, and the elphs walked solemnly to the fireplace, circling it. Then their voices rose into the air:

> *We call you all, come hear our call,*
> *The Council meets, come one, come all.*
>
> *As you slip and slide along,*
> *Listen to our mournful song.*
> *Stolen was one of your kind,*
> *In a lonely cell confined.*
>
> *Wronged you are, and now we'll see*
> *The culprits punished fittingly.*
> *We will lend you tongue and voice,*
> *Be the judges, make the choice.*

We call you all, we call you all,
The Council meets, come here, come all.

As they sang, the bindervines creaked and swayed. Bill's feet and hands were numb from the vines' tight grip, the swaying was making him feel sick, and he really didn't like the sound of the part about 'punishment'. He closed his eyes, willing the sick feeling to go away, but when he opened them again, it seemed to be getting worse. The grass below was smudged and blurred, and slightly sparkly. He blinked again and again, trying to see clearly, and then he saw them.

There was nothing wrong with his eyes. The clearing was covered in trails of slime, left there by hundreds of snails. There were golden ones, like the one the green knight had found, but mingled among them were fat brown snails with huge squat shells on their backs, blue ones flecked with orange, and strange colourless ones with pink eyes and transparent shells. Within moments every blade of grass had been flattened, and the whole clearing was coated in slime. Yet more kept emerging from the forest, and soon the ground was an oozing mass of snails, gliding noiselessly over one another.

Bill shuddered, and found himself feeling unexpectedly grateful that the bindervines were holding him up in the air. A muffled whistle cut across the clearing, and he grimaced at the sight of Whistler's bony feet, glistening with slime. The three elphs were ankle-deep in it, but they seemed untroubled, and lifted their voices again:

Welcome to you who heard our call,
The Council meets, welcome to all.
We brought you here, we've done our part,
Now take our mouths, let justice start!

All three let their heads fall forward, as if they were asleep. Then Phlippa raised blank eyes to Bill, and began to speak. An utterly unfamiliar voice issued from her mouth: a wet, clotted voice that seemed to struggle for breath, as if it was drowning.

"You are the one they call Bill," said the voice.

"Yes," admitted Bill, nervously. "Um... how do you know that?"

Phenella lifted her head, and opened her mouth.

"He knows because that elph knows," said another voice, just as strange and sodden as the first, "just as I know the mind of this elph."

Phrank's head rose last.

"And I, this," gargled a third voice.

Bill stared at Phrank's pot belly, wondering if he should tell the elph that there was a fat brown snail crawling across his stomach. Then he realized that Phenella had a speckled blue snail in her hand, and a pale, transparent snail was making its slimy way down Phlippa's fuzzy green arm.

"You're the snails," said Bill, understanding. "If you're touching the elphs, you can talk through them."

"There is no need for you to speak," said the brown snail, through Phrank.

"We will use your mouth to hear the truth," said the transparent snail, through Phlippa.

"Use my mouth?" said Bill. "But how will…"

He caught sight of his scarf, and the words died in his throat. Slowly making its way up from the ground, over the coiling vines and the tufts of wool, was a golf ball-sized snail, with a shining golden shell.

Bill tried to shrink away from it, but the vines kept their grip on him. The snail went on oozing its way up the scarf. Its slick stomach glided onto a spring of his hair, sliding along the green tendril knotted into it. Bill clamped his eyes shut. Then he felt a cool, sticky sensation on his forehead, like a long and profoundly unwelcome kiss.

There was a noise in his head, a low bubbling sound. His throat suddenly felt tight. Then his mouth was opening, and he felt a voice issuing from deep within, sounding wet and strangled.

"This is the one who began the quest," it was saying. "This is the child."

Bill felt the snail gliding across his forehead and sliding slowly, moistly down his cheek.

"It does not seem to like our species much," the voice continued. "It fears I may slip into its ear, or its mouth, and it would not like that."

He desperately tried to empty his head of everything, to leave his mind a total blank, but the bubbling rose up again, and he realized it was laughter.

"Apparently it promises to put my slippers by the fire, for when I get home," the voice gurgled. "Though it wishes I had not told you that."

Bill felt his face grow hot, as the snail oozed onto his chin.

"And of the matter at hand?" said the clotted voice of the transparent snail.

Bill concentrated hard. There was no bubbling now.

"The child meant no harm," said the voice, eventually. "It did not know this would happen. And for my part, I was not injured by my captivity."

Bill struggled to speak again, trying to apologize, but the voice broke into his racing thoughts, and this time it spoke not through his mouth, but only in his head.

"Your elph friend was right about what has happened here, child," it said. "In our speechless state we could do nothing to prevent it. We live long lives; we see all things come and go, both good and evil. But this is a dark time. Your cause is just. We wish you strength, and luck."

Bill's mind tumbled over with questions, but as the snail glided up his other cheek, the voice clogged his throat again.

"The child has enough to worry it," the voice announced. "I see no need for further punishment."

Bill couldn't help screwing up his face in disgust as the golden snail made its leisurely way back across his forehead, but he got the strong impression the snail forgave him. As it began to slither along his hair, and back down his scarf, a shiver ran through him, as if he had briefly held something remarkable and ancient, only to lose it again a moment later.

"Here ends the Council," said the fat brown snail, gliding down Phrank's leg.

Bill watched as the speckled blue snail, and the transparent one, joined the oozing carpet of others on the ground. The elphs' heads fell forward, and then all three looked up at him, their eyes glossy with sorrow.

"Oh, Bill!" wailed Phenella.

"Oh, poor nice new friends," cried Phrank.

"Oh, and poor, poor elph," howled Phlippa, gazing up at Phly still smothered in her ball of vines.

"We're so sorry!" they chorused, letting tears run down their fuzzy faces.

"That's all right," said Bill, moving his jaw rather stiffly as the snail trail circling his face began to dry. "Really. It doesn't matter."

"Oh, but it does!" sang Phlippa.

"We tied you all up!" sang Phenella.

"We should have known better!" sang Phrank.

They joined hands, and moaned together.

"Honestly," said Bill, "it wasn't so bad. And the snails seem quite happy. So... do you think you could let us go now?"

The three river elphs began to hum at once, and the earth began to vibrate. The leafy coils that held his ankles began to loosen; the tendrils began to untwine themselves from his hair. He could hear the knights' armour creaking and unbuckling, over a relieved whistling sound. Tallulah's legs were now free enough to kick with, and Phly's ears were visible amidst the knotted vines, as Silva and the antelope were slowly lowered to the ground.

Bill reached for the ground with his newly free arm, but without warning a thick black bindervine snaked up from the earth, and gripped his wrist. He yelped in pain and surprise, as more swift black coils wrapped themselves around his shoulders and knees, wrenching him back into the air. Tallulah was trying to shout something, but black ropes silenced her. The river elphs' humming gave way to squeals of bewilderment, as vines twisted around their slender limbs. The flames of the campfire flickered wildly, then abruptly went out. The clearing was plunged into darkness.

He could still smell smoke, but it wasn't the aromatic wood smoke of the campfire. A freezing wind blew down from above, driving the oily stink of petrol towards him, burning his eyes. There were heavy footsteps in the trees.

Bright beams of light flooded down onto the camp. Bill blinked tears away, and looked up to see a black, bulging ship hovering above the clearing, belching clouds of smoke. Marching out of the trees were ranks of Gatherers, their filthy leather uniforms creaking as they filed two by two into the camp, their boots crunching snail shells with every step. Then they halted, and hundreds of blank, curving faces turned as one to face him.

A figure pushed through their ranks towards him, and Bill found himself looking into the smiling eyes of Owen Silva.

"Oh, no, Bill," he said, brushing his hair neatly back into place. "I don't plan on letting you go at all."

Chapter Thirteen

The Great Spondozo

... in which Bill finds himself at the centre of the
universe, and Whistler is surprised

Bill stumbled down a dark, dripping corridor,
and wished that it wasn't quite so familiar. Most schools
go on trips to zoos, or funfairs, but year after year
his school had taken them to an old coal mine in the
valleys of South Wales, to see whether they would have
liked to be a miner. Bill's answer had been a resounding
no; the hat with the lamp on the front was very
heavy, and some of the tunnels were so small that even
he had to bend his head to get through them. Worst of
all was the way little trickles of mud and dust dropped
from the roof girders, as if to remind you that you
were underground, and that at any moment half of
Wales might fall on your head and bury you. Now he
was walking through a very similar tunnel at the
centre of the universe, with the weight of every layer
pressing down on him from above. The familiarity was
not comforting.

The journey from Phly's world had seemed endless, and he had spent it in lonely silence, wedged between rows of huge, faceless guards. Now, as a Gatherer led them wordlessly on into the gloom, there was nothing left to do but wonder what grim fate awaited them. If Tallulah's half-hearted stomping and Phly's mournful hum were anything to go by, he wasn't the only one feeling anxious; Whistler, too, was walking with his head bowed, his wrinkled face in shadow. Perhaps, Bill thought, the roof caving in might not be so bad after all. At least the end would be quick.

Not everyone was so apprehensive. The antelope merely blinked as it trotted under the feet of the Gatherer bringing up the rear, impassive as ever, though Bill found the pattering of its hooves oddly comforting. Owen Silva wore a smirk of satisfaction as he strode confidently ahead. The three river elphs were skipping along quite cheerfully, wide-eyed with fascination at their new surroundings. And although the knights' shiny armour had been so crumpled by the bindervines that the lilac knight was limping, and one of the green knight's arms was twisted above his head as if he really wanted to answer a question, their spirits were undaunted.

"You'll never take us alive!" declared the rust-red knight, trying without success to pull his sword from its bent scabbard.

"You already have been taken alive, you fools," sneered Silva.

The lilac knight lifted his chin defiantly. "Well, we certainly shan't be telling you anything. Not even under pain of torture!"

"There won't actually be any torture, will there?" whispered the green knight.

Bill felt his throat tighten, and he looked at Tallulah. She looked pale, but shook her head.

"No one's going to torture you," she said. "You don't know anything useful."

"I know how to make daisy chains!" Phlippa piped up.

"And me! And me!" chorused Phrank and Phenella.

"I doubt they'll torture you for that," said Whistler, distantly.

"Although I might," murmured Tallulah.

Owen Silva cleared his throat, as the first Gatherer halted their march outside a mouldy-looking wooden door leading off the tunnel. "I assure you, ladies and gentlemen," said Silva, as the Gatherer drew out a bunch of keys and fitted them to the lock, "the Great Spondozo richly rewards those loyal to him. And he repays treachery with equal enthusiasm."

The wooden door swung open, to reveal a tiny, dank cell. Huddled against the back wall was a crowd of frightened figures, dressed in rags. They cowered at the sight of the Gatherer, their eyes stark white in their grubby faces.

"He must still be deciding what to do with these worthless renegades," said Silva, as the second Gatherer shoved the three knights unceremoniously into the cell. "But trust me, you three won't be kept waiting too long. For what you did to me, I'll personally see to it that you get preferential treatment."

Silva turned to continue down the corridor with

a smirk, but his face fell as the Gatherer placed a huge gloved hand on his chest, and pushed. Silva toppled backwards, and landed, hard, on the sprawled knights.

"Wait!" he shouted, struggling to his feet. "Stop, you imbeciles, I'm not one of them! I'm on your side!"

The silent Gatherers ignored him, and slammed the door in his face. As they ushered their captives on down the tunnel, Bill could hear Silva's fists pummelling the wood.

"I don't belong here!" he howled, in a muffled voice. "I'm a faithful servant of the Great – "

There was a clang, then a thud, and the howling ceased.

"I say, nice punch," came the faint voice of the green knight.

Tallulah raised an eyebrow. "If that's the rich reward, I hate to think what they do to…" She tailed off, as Phly shivered. "Sorry," muttered the princess. "I'll shut up now."

Bill stared down the damp tunnel. Set into the walls were more rotting wooden doors: hundreds of them. Behind each one, he realized, there was probably another tiny cell, filled with grimy, hopeless faces.

"Ooh, I hope we get a dungeon as mouldy as that one!" sang Phlippa brightly.

Phrank clapped his hands. "All those new friends to meet!"

"We could teach everyone new songs all day!" sang Phenella, hopping up and down.

At the next door, the three elphs were shoved into another gloomy little cell. Phly gave them a mournful wave goodbye, but by the time the key turned in the lock, they were already chanting endless hellos, and launching into a new song, called 'I like slime, it's easy to rhyme', accompanied by Phrank on the beard-banjo.

Bill felt a heavy hand pushing him forward, and stumbled unwillingly on, the antelope close on his heels. As they approached the next wooden door, Tallulah glanced furtively over her shoulder at the guard behind them. "Hey, Bill," she hissed, "If you were thinking of using that Plan, now would probably be a good time?"

"Ooh, are we doing the Plan now?" sang Phly, suddenly sounding more hopeful.

"Shh!" said Whistler, giving her a warning look. Neither of the Gatherers seemed concerned, which Bill thought to himself rather sadly was fair enough, since there was no Plan, and never had been.

He opened his mouth to admit as much, but the Gatherer in front led them on, past the next cell.

"Where are we going?" whispered Bill, wondering why *not* being locked in a tiny dungeon had suddenly begun to seem so alarming.

Tallulah shrugged bleakly, as they carried on past door after door. The tunnel was growing lower and narrower, and they spread out into single file. The doors stopped appearing at intervals along the walls. Bill found himself walking with his chin tucked in and his shoulders a little stooped, like those pictures of human ancestors who were not quite monkeys any more, but not quite men either. From the groaning whistle coming from the tall alien, Whistler was struggling with the close fit, while Tallulah muttered various rude words under her breath, as she scraped her elbows on the rough, muddy walls.

When the tunnel had shrunk to a size that only the elph and the antelope were comfortable with, the Gatherer in front halted. They had arrived at a miniature door, like a cat-flap for an unusually large cat. The Gatherer unlocked it, then turned awkwardly around, grabbed Bill, and shoved him through the doorway between his legs. Tallulah, Phly, Whistler (with some difficulty), and last the antelope, were pushed through after him. Then, without a word, the door was slammed closed, and the key turned in the lock.

To Bill's surprise, they were not in a dungeon, but a large, warm room, with plenty of space to breathe and very little visible reason for the roof to suddenly crumble and fall on your head. The risk of something *else* falling on your head was, however, substantial, for the place was stacked floor to ceiling with what Bill could only describe as *stuff*, all of it covered in a thick layer of dust. There were square cardboard boxes covered in brown paper, piled haphazardly on top of one another. Balls of wool, and curled sheets of yellowed paper, and ice-cube trays jostled with cracked wine glasses, and crumpled dried flowers, and foreign coins with the shine gone off them. Hatboxes tied with faded ribbon lined a rickety row of shelves up one wall. Shoeboxes, bulging at the sides, threatened to leak seashells and elegant perfume bottles onto the floor. A bundle of tattered cloth was draped over an oddly-shaped, ornamental wooden chair, with huge carved arms like banister posts; beside it was what looked at first like a harp, but turned out to be half of a grand piano, turned on its side and warping slowly in the dry warmth.

The antelope trotted forward, weaving between piles of old photograph albums and towers of books, but even its delicate steps were enough to dislodge a framed portrait of someone who looked faintly queenly from its resting place on a chest of drawers. It fell forwards, the glass smashing into tiny fragments. Phly jumped at the noise, and her head hit a shelf above her, tipping a jar of something pale pink, powdery and slightly perfumed all over her head. The elph sneezed musically, and rubbed her fuzzy skin, sending clouds of the pink powder up into the air and making them all cough.

"Stop it, Phly," Tallulah whispered. The room was so eerily quiet, it seemed somehow wrong to speak normally.

The elph sneezed again. "Sorry," she sang, trying to hold her nose with a hand that was more dusty than her head, and sneezing a third time.

They stayed huddled by the tiny door, not daring to move.

"What is this place?" murmured Bill. "Some sort of storeroom?"

Tallulah shrugged. "It's not exactly your typical dungeon," she whispered.

Behind him, Bill heard a low whistle. Whistler pushed past them and headed to a far corner of the room, kicking dusty objects out of his way as if he couldn't see them.

"Easy, Whistler, mate!" said Tallulah, the need to be respectfully quiet rapidly disappearing as the floor creaked, and small avalanches started all around the room. But Whistler kept moving. Propped in a corner was a large object with a curving outline. A piece of embroidered fabric had been thrown over it like a tarpaulin, and the alien began to tear it away, raising billows of dust. As the air cleared, the object was revealed: a shape like a fat pointed bullet, as tall as the room, with a sheen that hinted it might once have been shiny.

Whistler stood back, whistling softly with a gleam in his yellow eyes. He beamed at them, standing back from the shape with his arm outstretched, as if expecting a round of applause.

Bill, Tallulah and Phly stared back, bewildered.

Whistler huffed, and grabbed the cloth, polishing an area of the dusty surface until it began to glow silver. Bill turned his head to one side, realising something was printed there.

"Brian IV," he read out loud, and frowned. He recognized the name, but he couldn't remember where he'd heard it before.

"Yes!" whooped Whistler. "I knew you'd understand!"

"For those of us who don't speak Weirdo," Tallulah said, pointedly raising an eyebrow, "what the pilf is a Brian IV?"

"Not *a* Brian IV," said Whistler. "*The* Brian IV. The one and only. This..." He broke off, stroking a bony hand across the lettering, and taking a deep, solemn breath before continuing. "This ship belonged to Gregorius Antenmann, the greatest explorer who ever lived."

Bill nodded slowly. It looked just as he'd always imagined a spaceship should, before he'd seen a

Mercuroid: like a rocket, with a pointed nose cone, and three fins at the base allowing it to stand upright.

"It's very lovely," sang Phly, clapping her hands and surrounding herself in a pink cloud.

"Way to go, Whistler," said Tallulah sardonically. "You found a broken spaceship belonging to some dead guy. Can we start looking for a way out now?"

Whistler stared at her, dumbstruck. "You don't understand," he said, shaking his head. "This is *Antenmann's* ship. He designed it. He built it himself. This is the ship he travelled in on his last great expedition!"

"It's very, *very* lovely," sang Phly earnestly.

Whistler sighed. "Maybe you'll have to see inside to fully appreciate it," he said, wiping down more of the silver surface and locating a studded metal hatch in the side. He grabbed the handle and twisted it, struggling against rust and dust, until the hatch swung open with a groan. Closing his eyes briefly, as if to savour the moment, he climbed inside. Then he gasped.

"It's still here," he breathed, reverently running his hands over a large square box that protruded from the wall, with the letters AND stamped upon it. "The first... the original..."

"Ooh," sang Phly, who had climbed onto Tallulah's shoulders to see, and was managing to stay upright by knotting her small fingers into the tangled mop of hair.

"What's the big deal?" said Tallulah, trying unsuccessfully to unseat the elph. "The one in the egg was invisible. I mean, that's got to be better, right?"

Whistler shook his head, unable to tear his eyes from the device. "You don't understand. Antenmann's

Navigational Destinator is simply a device that makes travel between the layers possible. It will travel quite randomly, unless programmed with precise destination data. Of course, this one was only the prototype: history suggests it travelled quite randomly even *with* precise destination data. But over the centuries since he disappeared, scientists as brilliant as Antenmann himself have continued his research. The AND you'll find in a Mercuroid – in any ship – is now far more accurate."

"So this is just a worthless piece of junk?" said Tallulah.

"No, no, you're not listening!" said Whistler, flapping his hands. "Antenmann theorised that it was possible to create a Perfect AND: an AND that could take you anywhere, in the blink of an eye. It would require two things: first, a fully-functioning, totally accurate Navigational Destinator. And second, a map of every single layer of the universe, to provide the destination data. That's what the Expeditioners' League was set up to do: to gather data for the map. Of course, when Antenmann disappeared, we didn't just lose the genius most likely to build the first totally accurate Navigational Destinator. We lost all the destination data that he had downloaded onto the very first AND."

Whistler traced the lettering on the box with a shaky finger. "With that data, Antenmann dreamed of piecing together the ultimate map... creating an AND that could *control* the rotations... a device that could let you travel anywhere..."

"I didn't just dream about it, you young fool," said a brittle, withered voice behind them. "I made it possible."

Bill whirled around, and screamed. Towering above them, and staring from sunken yellow eyes, was a grotesque figure. Never, even in his cruellest nightmares, had Bill seen anything so freakishly hideous. There was no doubt he was a Quxynggrotly, like Whistler. But while Whistler's head was small and wrinkly, like a pickled walnut, this ancient alien's was so shrivelled it was barely there at all. His arms and legs had wasted away to sticks, and the dungarees he wore (like Whistler's, with silver embroidery on the front pocket, only the cloth was a very faded, well-washed green) flapped around him like an old skin. He looked so close to death, if not already beyond it, that he had been in the room all the time, so still and lifeless that they'd mistaken him for a bundle of rags on a carved wooden chair. In fact, his aged limbs were no longer able to support his weight, for it was the chair that was making him stand; his skeletal wrists and ankles were strapped onto the wooden arms and legs, and skilful engineering allowed the chair to unfold itself and draw him upright. He gazed down at them from those terrible yellow eyes, and laughed, a long, thin, papery scrape of a laugh, creaking from ill-used lungs, and rasping on long after their screaming had died.

Bill tore his gaze away, and saw that Tallulah was white-faced and trembling. Phly had buried her face in the princess' neck, and was peeping one wide and frightened eye over her shoulder, her cloak tinkling as she quivered. Even the antelope was standing stock still, staring at Antenmann with wide brown eyes.

"Gregorius Antenmann," breathed Whistler, in a whisper so faint it raised no dust.

The shrivelled face twisted into a gruesome representation of a smile.

Tallulah swallowed noisily, and shook her head. "No," she said, her voice sounding oddly smothered. "The Great Spondozo."

The sunken yellow eyes blazed with pleasure for a moment, and Bill saw Whistler's face crumple, as the boyish excitement that had flowed from him was snuffed out like a matchstick under a tidal wave.

Antenmann grasped the rounded ends of the carved arms of his chair with pale, bulgy knuckles, and rasped out a cackle. The chair flexed beneath him to allow him to lean forward a little, as if he were bent double with laughter, and then it folded itself back into a seated position, placing him on a level with Tallulah's eyes.

"The Great Spondozo?" he croaked, fixing her with his yellow gaze. "Me? My dear child, why ever would you think such a thing?"

Tallulah drew her head back, as if afraid of his breath. "This is the c-centre of the universe," she said shakily, "Where the Great Spondozo lives and… and builds his evil armies."

"Captures people and makes them his slaves," piped Phly nervously, in a discordant chime that sent a shiver up Bill's spine.

"And is always looking," said Whistler, in a desolate voice, "for ways to control the layers."

Antenmann sniffed, the creased flaps of skin around his gills fluttering repulsively. "I suppose I am guilty of that last one, yes," he said slowly.

Whistler's eyes filled with tears. "The finest theoretician there ever was," he said. "The greatest explorer that ever fell down a hole in the ground and lived to tell the tale. I wrote essays about your travels in school. I had posters of you on my bedroom wall! I became an expeditioner because I wanted to be... just like you!"

Bill watched, mortified, as large tears rolled down Whistler's face and plopped into the Brian IV. Antenmann merely pursed his barely-there lips, and smiled thinly.

"Did you now?" he said, reedily. "Is that why you're wearing the *orange* dungarees?"

Whistler's grey face paled, and a low whistle escaped from his gills.

"Whistler?" said Tallulah, frowning at him.

Whistler looked at her, and then at all of them, with desolation in his eyes. "I was going to tell you," he said, quietly. "Really, I was. But you were all being so nice to me, and I just... it never really seemed the right..." He sighed. "I didn't know how," he said, looking at his feet.

"Didn't know how to tell us what?" said Tallulah.

"That I've been lying to you," said Whistler, guiltily. "From the moment we met."

Bill felt his heart skip in his chest. Suddenly everything began to fall into place. Whistler had been more than happy to take them to Phly's world, and the Gatherers had turned up only hours later. Back on the landing platform in Quxyng, he'd nearly confessed something terrible. And now Bill realized the awful truth. *The Great Spondozo has spies everywhere*: the alien had said it himself. Bill had just never imagined how true that might turn out to be.

"I know," said Bill, his voice catching in his throat as he saw the shamed look on Whistler's face. "I know what you are."

Whistler nodded miserably. "Yes," he said. "I'm a catering assistant."

Bill blinked in confusion.

"You're a *what*?" said Tallulah loudly, forgetting Antenmann entirely and putting her hands on her hips.

"I'm not the Lord High Expeditioner, I'm a catering assistant. I did go on the last expedition from Quxyng, but I… I mostly made the tea and did the washing-up." Whistler hung his head.

"Um," said Bill, feeling relieved and more than a little guilty; reading so many stories had obviously made him suspicious. "That doesn't sound so bad."

Whistler shook his head. "That's not all," he said, delving into the front pocket of his dungarees, and removing the flat square of silver. "The Knowletron. I… I stole it."

"Oh," said Bill.

"I didn't mean to," said Whistler helplessly. "Not permanently, anyway."

The tearful alien explained how he had become disillusioned with life aboard their ship, the Alison VI. The real Lord High Expeditioner had successfully navigated his way through countless holes, charting new worlds, and being attacked by oddly-shaped new creatures daily. But Whistler saw nothing of this, trapped in the ship's kitchen. He longed for a taste of adventure, and so hatched a Plan: he would deliver the hovertrolley of tea as usual, casually pick up the Knowletron while passing through the Lord High Expeditioner's cabin, and then, while everyone was asleep, dash off into the nearest forest and discover something new, significant, and preferably not hungry. He would be back before anyone knew he was gone, having made the finest discovery of the whole mission.

"Don't tell me: they left without you," said Tallulah.

Whistler sighed, and nodded. "There I was, with no ship, no crew, nothing but the Knowletron. I couldn't go home; they'd think I was a thief, or some sort of spy."

Bill coughed uncomfortably.

"The first city I found, people just assumed I was on an expedition. I thought I might as well add to the Knowletron while I was there: fascinating place, quite wet, but really rather beautiful. Their ecosystem was the most... wait, here, let me show you."

The alien's tear-stained face brightened a little, as he gently, reverentially pressed a small button on the front of the Brian IV's AND. A tray slid out, and he placed the open Knowletron into it. At once the familiar revolving globe of light appeared, this time larger, and brighter. Whistler spun his finger through the globe, revealing images of writhing eel-like creatures, and vast caverns underwater, and the trailing seaweed hair of what looked to Bill like mermaids. With each new image Whistler gave a little gasp, like a proud mother over a photograph album. His eyes filled with fresh tears at the memories, and he turned away.

"It just sort of carried on from there," he sniffed, wiping a damp hand over his head. "By the time I ended up in that dungeon with you, I was so used to being an Expeditioner, I didn't have the heart to tell you the truth."

"You great prawn," said Tallulah, breaking into a grin. "We wouldn't have minded."

Phly leaned into the Brian IV from Tallulah's shoulder, and put a slender arm around Whistler's neck, rubbing her fuzzy head against his shoulder comfortingly. "I think you're lovely, whatever you are," she hummed. "And you *are* an Expeditioner."

"You didn't really steal the Knowletron," said Bill. "Well, you did... but you were going to put it back."

Whistler's face wrinkled up into a smile, but before he could speak there was a loud, scratchy noise from behind them.

"Ahem," said Gregorius Antenmann, clearing his papery throat. "You know, since it's stolen property, you really ought to give that Knowletron to me."

Bill stared at the ancient Quxynggrotly. The sunken yellow eyes had a new, hungry glint in them. He followed their ardent gaze, and caught a glimpse of the globe of light hovering over the AND in the Brian IV. It had grown brighter still, and within it he could now see tiny hoops of golden light, spinning and sparking within one another. But the globe disappeared, as Whistler snapped the Knowletron shut.

"You don't deserve to have it any more than me," said Whistler, bitterly. "To think I dedicated my life to following in the footsteps of the mighty Antenmann, when all the time he was the Great Spondozo."

"I'm not, you know," croaked the dry voice.

"Not what?" said Tallulah, rudely.

"I'm not the Great Spondozo."

Bill stared at the terrible, shrunken alien, and shuddered at the prospect of someone even more terrifying.

"So you aren't perfecting an AND so that you can control all the layers?" said Whistler.

"Ah," rasped Antenmann. "Well. Technically speaking, yes, I am doing that."

Under Whistler's appalled gaze, Antenmann leaned back against the carved wood as if it were a deck chair, and tried to look innocent. "What's a Lord High Expeditioner to do?" he rasped. "Every time you come home it's nag, nag, nag. When's your next expedition, Gregorius? Have you invented a new kind of spaceship yet? They want your picture, they want your autograph, they want to hear wild and wonderful stories of the fantastic places you've seen, and for you to sound just as excited as you did when you told the story for the very first time."

Whistler blinked, a faraway look on his face as if he were imagining such a life.

"I'm a scientist," wheezed Antenmann. "I don't like people, I like numbers and bits of machinery. Working down here in the museum, it's the only time in my life I've been left in peace to continue my research. And I've done it. A perfect, fully-functioning AND, just waiting for a perfect map to complete it. If it falls into the hands of the Great Spondozo, so be it. Someone's got to have it. Why not her?"

"*Her?*" said all four of them at once.

Antenmann hissed out a breath. "Oh, yes. She doesn't put it about that she's a lady, of course. People just don't seem to be quite so frightened of female evil geniuses."

Bill bit his lip, and thought that perhaps more people ought to meet his granny.

"Oh, she's not that bad, you know," Antenmann croaked, a hint of a smile on his wizened lips. "Horrifyingly insane, perhaps, but not really evil. And in her current state, she's completely harmless. Would you like to meet her?"

~★~

The room was so full of rubbish that even Gregorius Antenmann, who appeared to have been asleep in it for several years, had difficulty finding the way out. The antelope eventually found a round wooden door hidden behind a dressing-table with a wobbly leg. Antenmann gripped the arms of his chair, and its carved wooden feet rose and fell, propelling him to the door with a rocking, unsteady gait.

Bill, Tallulah, Phly, Whistler, and the antelope followed him through the circular opening, into a room so staggeringly strange that Bill felt dizzy just looking at it. He dropped onto his knees at once in alarm, for the floor was not flat, and seemed to carry on all the way around the perfectly spherical room. There was no ceiling; there were no walls; there was only an endless floor curving up all around him, leaving him not entirely sure which way was up. If he crawled forwards, his hands and feet stayed on the ground, but if he looked straight up, there was the floor still up above him, and everything that was up there showed no sign of dropping on his head.

Bill felt very relieved about that, for there were an awful lot of things up there. There were an awful lot of things everywhere. Almost every part of the creaky, wooden floor was covered in large cabinets, with wooden sides and glass fronts, and rows of shallow drawers; every cabinet was stuffed full from top to bottom. The narrow paths weaving between the cabinets were broken every few feet by round wooden doors painted in faded colours, deep red, dark green, midnight blue; every door led off, Bill guessed, to another cluttered room like Antenmann's. Despite the vastness of the space, and the mustiness of the air, the whole room had a homely, familiar feel, perhaps from the globe of golden light that hung in the centre of the room like a pale sun, casting a soft glow over everything.

Immediately to Bill's left was a long glass case, packed with dolls, train sets, wooden building blocks, counters from board games, paper money, and hundreds of other small objects Bill couldn't identify, as if someone had picked up a toy shop and emptied it out like a piggy bank. Another, taller cabinet on his right held rows of bottles, with labels too dusty to read, filled with colourful liquids. Next to every object, or hanging from it on a little thread, was a tiny yellowed piece of card, with minute handwriting on it in brown ink.

"Welcome," croaked Antenmann, "to the Museum."

Bill cautiously got to his feet. That was what was familiar; that hushed atmosphere, as if the air was thicker than usual, and people swam slowly through it, their voices slightly muffled. Bill had been taken to a few museums by his mum and dad, and although his parents always wanted to spend ages in the boring sections and hurry through the good bits, all three of them rather enjoyed putting imaginary flesh on the dinosaur bones and scaring themselves. Bill was less fond of the stuffed animals, who always had legs at funny angles, and wonky glass eyes frozen in a slightly embarrassed expression.

"What sort of museum?" said Bill, stepping tentatively over a faded red door towards a case full of peculiar glass tubes, springs and wires.

"Remarkable," said Whistler, his gills quivering as he pressed his wrinkly face close to the glass. "A complete collection of early hyper-navigational modulators. This must be a museum of transport."

Bill looked over at the next case, which was even larger than the last, and saw it contained what looked like an entire double-decker bus.

"You're wrong," said Tallulah, who had wandered far enough away along the curved floor that to Bill she seemed to be leaning sideways, even though she was standing up straight. Before her was a tall, narrow cabinet filled with pieces of rusty metal. "Weaponry," she said, grinning. "This is a museum of war."

The antelope 'eef'ed from somewhere far above them, and Bill squinted past the glowing globe to catch a glimpse of a pointy horn hanging upside down.

A mournful chiming sound drew him back to the double-decker bus. Phly's eyes were brimming over with tears as she touched the glass with a fuzzy finger, and

Bill hurried over, careful to dodge the wooden doors in the floor in case they burst open beneath him. The elph crawled up into his arms and wrapped herself around him, sobbing into his scarf.

"Nasty museum of horrible," she sniffed.

Bill gazed into the cabinet, and saw that this was the sort of museum he didn't like. Sitting stiffly in the seats of the bus were stuffed animals with staring glassy eyes: goats, and chickens, and zebras who didn't have enough room and had hooked their legs over the seat in front. There were other animals too that Bill didn't know: things a bit like llamas only with too many heads, purple things with curly arms like monkeys' tails, and birds that looked like big balls of fluff.

"It's not *a* museum of anything," said Antenmann reedily, his wooden chair creaking and stomping its way up the wall. "It's *the* museum. *Every* museum. This," he said, pausing for a wheezing breath, "is the Big Museum of Things."

As he spoke, wooden doors all around the room flapped open like a series of cuckoo clocks, teasingly flinging a hint of themselves into the room before snapping shut again. Bill heard snatches of music, half-remembered songs; smells floated into the air, of mown grass and peanut butter and barbecues; rainbows of light flooded the space, and flashed away in seconds. Everywhere he looked, a door was closing and another opening, thick and fast, overlapping in a great cacophony of sound and smell and memory, until, with the bang of the last door, the room fell silent.

"Blimey," murmured Bill.

"The finest collection ever conceived," croaked Antenmann, his chair still thumping its way between the endless glass cabinets. "A museum that contains *everything*. Including…"

The carved feet of Antenmann's chair thudded to a halt in front of a case made entirely of glass, with plush red lining on the floor.

"… its creator."

They all gathered around the case, staring at it with open mouths.

Inside the glass cabinet, standing on the red plush like a very ugly mannequin in a shop window, was a stout old woman with a slight hunch, and her grey hair scraped off her face in a tight bun. A grim whisper of a smile puckered her wrinkled face; her eyes, one cloudy and blind, the other steely grey, stared out at them unseeingly. By her foot, resting on the plush, was a small yellow placard.

"Exhibit No. 1 from level 56: Miss Adelaide Buckfast," read Whistler, kneeling before the case. "Also known as The Great Spondozo, Creator and Curator of the BMT."

"That's the Great Spondozo?" said Tallulah, wrinkling up her nose. "That's the evil supervillain? A dead woman in a glass box?"

Bill shuddered at the thought that someone might stuff an actual person and put them in a museum.

Antenmann let out a feeble sigh, and gazed at the woman in the case. "She told me it started with stamps," he said. "When she'd collected all of them, it was shoes, then string, then packets of sugar. Her mother, I believe, was the one who suggested she try books. A terrible mistake. The perfect library; every book ever written, amassed in a tower that brushed the clouds, on the patio in her back garden. Too heavy, you see. She placed the last book on the top shelf, and it fell straight through the ground, all the way to the centre of the universe."

Bill was just thinking that he'd rather like to have a library with every book ever written in it on his back porch, when the antelope brushed against his leg and stepped on his toe. It nudged Whistler aside, exposing a small lever in the wooden base of the cabinet. With a flick of its hoof, it deftly slid the lever across, then trotted backwards, and blinked.

A humming noise filled the air, as a purple glow flooded the glass cabinet. The front pane of glass swung open, and, to Bill's utter horror, the frozen whispery smile on the old woman's face melted away as she stepped forward, and fixed him with her mismatched eyes.

Chapter Fourteen

The Collection

*... in which Bill discovers
just how important he isn't*

"Hello, dear," the old woman said hoarsely, stooping to pat the antelope's head while staring at Bill through that strange, clouded eye. "You must be Bill."

Bill gazed at her with his mouth open. She hadn't leapt from the shadows like Antenmann, making them all scream. She didn't have a flowing black cloak, or a scar across her cheek. She didn't look like an evil supervillain at all. She was a just little old lady in a cardigan and a tweed skirt, who smelt of perfume and powder and looked like she might enjoy flower arranging. Looking miserably at the antelope, Bill reminded himself that sometimes appearances could be deceptive.

The antelope blinked at him coolly, apparently untouched by Bill's look of disappointment.

"Um," said Bill, remembering he'd been spoken to, and wishing his voice didn't sound so wobbly. "Yes."

"What do you want with Bill?" said Whistler,

drawing his shoulders back and doing his best to sound masterful over the faint whistle of terror that was flowing from his gills.

"Yeah, what makes him so special?" said Tallulah.

The old woman's translucent cheeks curved into a smile. "Nothing at all," she said.

Bill looked at his shoes, and buried his nose in the warm folds of his scarf. She was right, he thought mournfully. People said it all the time, and it was true.

Phly wrapped her fuzzy arms around his leg, but it didn't make him feel any better.

"But... but you had him kidnapped..." said Tallulah.

"You sent those wasps after him," said Whistler.

"And the Gatherers," hummed Phly from Bill's leg.

The old woman nodded, the bun on her head bobbing up and down. "I did indeed," she croaked. "Building a museum such as this is hardly a straightforward matter. You have to take over an entire layer to be absolutely certain you've got at least one of everything. But young Bill here happens to come from one of the layers I've yet to take over. Until I do, I have to make do with what falls down the holes. And my Big Museum of Things wouldn't be complete without a man, now, would it?"

Bill stared at the Great Spondozo, and bit his lip.

"But I'm not a man," he said hesitantly. "I'm a boy."

Spondozo sighed. "Yes, that's what those stupid rats thought. Held you up to the measuring stick, and dropped you straight onto the reject pile, without a thought of what you might grow up to be." She surveyed him with her good eye, looking him up and down. "I can see how that might have happened. But of course, by the time the paperwork came through, you'd already managed to escape."

"So that's why you've been chasing him?" said Tallulah, staring around at the cases and the wooden doors. "So you can stick him in a box in your freaky museum?"

"Good heavens, no," said Spondozo, much to Bill's relief. She began walking stiffly down one of the narrow passages between cases, the antelope trotting obediently at her heels. "You weren't the only one to slip through the net, young man. Fortunately for me, the hole from that layer opens up rather frequently. And those rats really aren't very bright."

They followed her, Antenmann's chair clumping noisily behind, until she halted before a particularly large display case with very thick glass. A metal plaque on the wooden base read 'Ripening'.

Bill gasped. The case was as crammed full of things as the other cabinets, but these things were moving. Large rabbity creatures, like guinea pigs with donkey ears, hopped across tufty squares of turf. Tiny salamanders flicked their tongues as they darted down the slender trunks of saplings. Beside a small pool sat a tiny blue girl with a row of knobbly horns poking from the top of her head, and a small figure dressed in grey, playing a game of cards without much enthusiasm.

"They're alive," breathed Bill, as the grey figure and the blue girl spotted them, and walked to the front of the case. As they emerged from the shadows, Bill saw the grey figure was a boy, tall, about twelve years old, with tousled blond hair and a suntanned face. He was wearing a small peaked cap, a grey blazer, a striped tie and long shorts.

"Graham!" sang Phly, detaching herself from Bill's leg and skipping to the glass to press her fuzzy nose against it.

The boy smiled, and moved his hands down the glass, as if he was trying to stroke her face. His lips moved, and he seemed to be explaining something to the blue girl.

"Of course," said Tallulah, waving at the boy. She nudged Bill. "He was the boy who fell down the hole before you."

"It means waiting ten years or so for them to be ready," said the Great Spondozo, admiring her specimens. "But in the long run, I think it pays to plan things in advance."

Bill swallowed, staring at Graham. "So… so you're just going to keep him in there, locked in that case for… for ten years?"

Spondozo smiled thinly. "Good practice for him. The others had to adjust to their new, still life just like *that*," she said, clicking two gnarled fingers.

"The others?" said Bill. Behind him, he heard the soft whine of Whistler's gills rising in pitch.

"Of course," said the old woman, gesturing stiffly at the thousands of display cases lining the curving walls. "This is a living museum. There's no point in collecting one of everything if they're all dead and crumbling to dust, is there?"

Bill turned, and looked into the nearest cabinet. Rows of glassy eyes stared back. In the next, crammed in with some boating equipment, he could make out more; and the next, and the next. In every single cabinet there were people, creatures, beings, frozen in odd postures like people unexpectedly photographed. All gazing out at him, silently watching.

Bill turned his face away. It was the most breathtakingly horrible fate he could imagine. He found himself clenching his fists, and wriggling his toes, just to remind himself that he still could.

"Obviously I've had to stop the ageing process, or I'd have to keep finding replacements, and you can imagine how much more time that might take," said Spondozo, cackling as if she expected them to share the joke. "The collection's taking so long to put together, I've had to put myself into the time freezer once or twice. By rights, Antenmann over there should have died about seven centuries ago, but his research into navigating the holes was vital to me. And where better to do research than sitting in a glass case for a few decades, with nothing to do but gather dust and think a lot?"

"You allowed that?" said Whistler to his former idol, shocked.

The back of Antenmann's chair lifted his bony shoulders into a shrug. "I'd never have finished it otherwise," he rasped. "And it was very peaceful," he added, "except when you got an itchy nose."

"After all that hard work, I was hardly going to let one boy ruin everything, was I?" said Spondozo, staring at Bill and pursing her lips.

Bill gazed up at her, confused. "But I haven't done anything," he said.

The old woman gave him a withering look. "Didn't escape from my dungeon, did you? Didn't remind those knights there was more to life than Cheese Beer, didn't set all those bank workers free?" She bore down on him, her croaking voice growing stronger. "I already had Graham by then, I didn't need you for my museum, but there you were again at that pathetic little peace conference, plotting against me! I'm sure outwitting that fool Owen Silva wasn't too taxing – but my wasps? An entire Gatherer assault squadron? My spy brought you a Mercuroid programmed to come directly to me, and you still got away. Who knows what kind of elph army you might have created if I left you in that horrible leafy place? If I hadn't had a spy working so close to you, you could have defeated me completely!"

The old woman held her powdered face so close to Bill's he could see the traces of pink lipstick that were bleeding into the wrinkles around her puckered little mouth. "But you failed," she spat. "I am the greatest collector the universe will ever know, and no one will ever take that away from me!"

Bill shrank back, bewildered.

"Excuse me," sang a small, musical voice down near his knees.

Bill looked down, and saw Phly tugging at the hem of the old woman's tweedy skirt.

"Excuse me," sang Phly again, very softly, "But I think you're wrong. You aren't the greatest collector ever, and your museum will never have everything in it."

"Child," spat Spondozo, looking at the elph as if she were something unpleasant stuck to her shoe. "This is the Big Museum of Things. I labelled every item, I locked every case. My Gatherers will continue to collect the exhibits. With Gregorius' help, their ships will eventually travel to every layer, until I control them all! And then my collection will be the greatest achievement in history!"

Phly's earrings jingled in the force of Spondozo's reply, but the elph stood firm. "Some things you can't lock in cases and put labels on," she sang softly. "Some things aren't meant to be tied down, they just are, like... like feelings."

A thoughtful silence settled over the room. Then it was broken by Tallulah making loud retching noises. "Phly," she said, wrinkling up her face in disgust, "I know you're a soppy little elph, but can you warn me next time you're going to say something that... that... *revoltingly sugary?*"

Phly looked down. "But it's true," she murmured, swishing her mossy robe around her feet.

Tallulah scratched her nose, chewed the inside of her cheek, and sighed. "Yeah, all right. It's true. Sappy and girly and utterly nauseating, but true." She grinned crookedly at the Great Spondozo. "You know what? Your collection sucks."

"Silence, girl!" said Spondozo, staring at the princess with distaste. "There is nothing my museum cannot contain! Name it! Name one thing!"

Tallulah wrinkled her nose, scraped the toe of her boot on the floor, and muttered something inaudible under her breath.

"Didn't quite catch that, dear," said Spondozo.

Tallulah glared at her from under her hair.

"Love," she said, grudgingly.

The Great Spondozo cast her eyes across the spherical room, then waved her hand in the air. A round wooden door flew open with a bang, and a shower of pink confetti flew into the air. Delicate harp music echoed round the museum. Through the doorway they could see a dimly-lit room, scattered with pink heart-shaped cushions, and photographs with lipstick kisses on them, and matching his and hers bathrobes, and boxes of chocolates, and huge bunches of long-stemmed red roses.

With a flick of Spondozo's wrist, the door slammed closed.

Tallulah stuck out her chin. "If that's your idea of love, you can keep it."

"I fully intend to," croaked the Great Spondozo. "Any other requests?"

Whistler cleared his throat. "The sub-atomic structure of a quark," he said proudly.

A second round door shot open near Whistler's feet. Bill peered into the dark space beneath. He couldn't see anything, but from the awed look on Whistler's face, whatever he'd requested seemed to be inside.

"You see?" croaked the old woman, as the door banged shut.

Phly looked pleadingly up at Bill.

"Um," said Bill, biting his lip. "What about Christmas?"

"Christmas?" the old woman spat. "Never heard of it! But I'll make sure it's the first thing I take, when I get to your world, young man. And believe me, it won't be long. Gregorius has completed his work on the AND. All I need now is a complete map of the layers, and my Gatherers shall be able to travel anywhere instantaneously!"

Bill caught the hungry gleam in Antenmann's eyes as they focused on Whistler's front pocket, and felt his stomach turn over.

"Not that you'll be around to see it," the old woman added, her lips puckering into a grim smile.

Bill swallowed, as Phly hid behind his leg. Tallulah defiantly put her hands on her hips, quivering very slightly; Whistler's gills began to whine. Even Antenmann shifted anxiously in his chair, the carved wooden feet shuffling him sideways as if they didn't want to be involved.

"You know, there's really no need to harm them," rasped the old Quxynggrotly, sounding vaguely shocked. His eyes flicked again to Whistler's pocket, as he jerkily retreated behind a display case.

Bill saw with relief that the bun on Spondozo's head was bobbing up and down as she nodded. "Indeed, Gregorius," the old woman said. "But it seems I can't trust them in an ordinary dungeon. And I already have a boy, a princess, an elph, and, thanks to you, a Quxynggrotly in my museum. So you see, there's really no need to keep them alive, either."

The Great Spondozo turned, and raised her arm. "Guards!" she croaked.

With a series of crashes, wooden doors all around the room flew open. And from the rooms beneath the museum, the Gatherers emerged. They crawled from the round doorways like beetles creeping out from under the skirting board, swarming into the room. Bill pressed his back against the nearest cabinet, edging away from an open door in the floor, as the huge faceless guards clambered out. They were centimetres away, their leather sleeves brushing against his face: he could feel Phly's tiny fingers gripping his ankle tighter and tighter as they strode past.

As one, the Gatherers halted.

"Kill them," said Spondozo. "Start with the little one."

Bill felt his knees weaken. He tried desperately to catch his breath, as the guards turned to face him. A piercing whistle rang through the air. He could hear Tallulah yelling something loud and possibly obscene. *Do something*, his brain was screaming, *do something, it doesn't matter what, just think of something…* Then the heavy hand of a Gatherer pushed him to the floor, and a leather gauntlet snatched at a rapidly retreating piece of green cloth.

"Help!" squeaked Phly, as she scrambled underneath a cabinet, rolling herself into a shivering, tinkling ball. Bill stared helplessly into her huge dark eyes, as more gloved hands groped for her. Then there was a thumping sound. With a crash something heavy landed on top of him, and everything went dark.

"Let her go, you filthy stinking pilfers!" bellowed a voice somewhere up above.

Bill writhed, and managed to free himself. Tallulah had flung herself onto the back of one of the guards, and had wrestled him to the floor, on top of Bill. She grabbed the trailing end of his scarf, and began to wrap it around the Gatherer's neck, yanking it tighter with every word.

"You... should leave... my friend... alone!"

The Gatherer rose unsteadily to his feet, Tallulah still clinging to his back, and slammed her against the cabinet. Bill heard the crack of her head connecting with the glass as he was swept off his feet by the tug on his scarf. He found himself sliding along the wooden floor into the feet of another Gatherer, who kicked him out of his path without a pause.

"Now, Adelaide," rasped Antenmann, stumping forward in his chair and fixing his yellow eyes on the princess's bloodied forehead. "I'm sure you don't... you can't... I mean to say, I don't believe resorting to violence is really..."

"Oh, I don't know, Gregorius," croaked the Great Spondozo, hanging upside down above them and craning her neck so she could watch. "After keeping still for so long, I find it all rather exhilarating." She chuckled, then drew a pair of half-moon spectacles from her cardigan pocket, and frowned. "That annoying little green thing isn't still alive, is it?"

Bill heard a musical whimper emerge from under the display case, and watched in horror as Gatherers lined up, preparing to tip it over. He could see Whistler dangling over a guard's shoulder, feebly kicking at the air. Tallulah was sitting up, touching her temple and staring at the blood on her fingers in confusion. Bill crawled to his knees, but was knocked to the floor again at once.

"I'm sorry, my children," muttered a rattling voice nearby. "But I can't allow this..."

Gregorius Antenmann drew a squat black box from his pocket, and gazed at it with the fuzzy bewilderment of someone who had only just woken up. He flipped it open to reveal a single red switch.

"What's that?" said Bill urgently.

"A Deactivator," Antenmann rasped. "I'm switching them off."

"Switching what off?" said Bill.

Antenmann looked around wistfully. "The Gatherers. *My* Gatherers."

Bill looked at the guards in confusion, noticing how they moved in perfect unison as they rocked the display case. The one nearest to him had torn the sleeve of his uniform, and under the leather Bill could see wires, and thick rods of black metal in place of bones.

"Robots," he murmured. "They're *robots*."

Antenmann closed his eyes. "Goodbye, my children," he whispered, raising a shaking, bony finger to the switch.

There was an appalling crash as the cabinet toppled over, its glass walls smashing into millions of pieces. Antenmann was flung from his chair, the Deactivator slipping from his grasp and skittering across the floor, skidding to a stop beside the Ripening case. Bill caught a glimpse of the silver fringe of Phly's cloak between the black boots of the guards closing in, and heard her wail in terror. Tallulah scrambled to her feet, and leapt desperately onto the back of one of the guards. Whistler lashed out wildly, swinging his bony fists and screeching out a high-pitched whistle. Antenmann reached out a skeletal hand, trying to drag his feeble frame towards the Deactivator, but it was too far.

The old Quxynggrotly fixed his sunken eyes on Bill. Bill knew what he had to do. Slipping on the broken glass, he struggled to his feet, and began to run towards the Deactivator. Somewhere up above him, he heard a tapping sound. From the other side of the museum the antelope was weaving its way through the cabinets, towards the Ripening case. Bill stumbled, his chest tightening as he almost fell through one of the round doorways. The antelope's hooves tapped faster. He ducked and twisted as Gatherers lumbered into his path, knocking him to his knees. The antelope leapt through the air, nimbly dodging another open doorway. The Ripening case was close now; the Deactivator was only feet away. Bill felt the blood pounding in his ears as he reached out a hand. Out of the corner of his eye he could see the swift blur of the antelope, moving in, jaws open. He stretched out his fingers, reaching, reaching…

His hand closed on the black box. The antelope's jaws closed on his hand.

Bill gasped, as the tiny pointed teeth pierced his skin. The antelope tugged, but he kept his grip on the Deactivator. He could hear screaming somewhere behind him, and the sound of something tearing. The antelope stared at him, unblinking. With a bitter sense of triumph, Bill raised his other hand, and pressed the switch.

Nothing happened.

Bill pressed it again, staring in panic as the Gatherers went on crowding round the toppled cabinet, ripping at something green and tinkling. He caught sight of Antenmann lying crookedly on the floor, gazing around in helpless confusion.

"Really, Gregorius," croaked the Great Spondozo from high above them. "Did you honestly think I wouldn't have deactivated your Deactivator?" She reached into the folds of her cardigan, and produced another squat black box. "*Mine* is the only one that works," she hissed.

Bill looked miserably at the useless black box in his hand. He'd done it. He'd got there first. He hadn't even fallen over. And it still hadn't made any difference.

"Enough playing," the old woman said. "I'm tired. I want to go back to being an exhibit. Guards, finish them off. All of them. Now."

The antelope sank its teeth further into Bill's hand. Inside the Ripening case, he could see Graham and the blue girl hammering noiselessly on the glass, shouting some kind of silent warning. He felt the floorboards shudder, and looked up to see two huge Gatherers bearing down on him.

"Let me go!" yelled Tallulah, as a leather-clad arm wrapped itself around her neck.

"Stop, please!" gasped Whistler, as his legs were pulled from under him, sending him crashing to the floor.

Bill wriggled frantically as two sets of heavy boots thumped towards him, and managed to free his injured hand, but the antelope pounced on him, pinning him down by the shoulders with its hard little hooves. The sharp teeth were snapping round his face, the pointy horns swiping at his cheek. The faceless guards drew nearer, close enough for him to hear the creaking of their leathers. Then the antelope bit down, going for Bill's throat, but the teeth closed on his scarf instead, and the creature staggered backwards, choking on fluffy strands of orange wool.

Bill rolled over, crawling away on his hands and knees, but a hand closed on his arm: a leather glove with a grip far stronger than any living thing could muster. He felt himself being lifted up and dangled in mid-air, as another hand closed around his neck. This time he knew the scarf wasn't going to save him. The mechanical fingers began to squeeze.

"Help... can't... breathe..." moaned Tallulah, her voice growing faint.

Bill gazed blearily at the antelope, which was still coughing up bits of fluff, frenziedly shaking its head from side to side. It made an odd snorting sound like a sneeze, gagged, then spat something small and metallic onto the floor.

Bill was dimly aware of a whirring sound. "Follooow..." it murmured, droning as if it were winding down. "Follooow the Greeeaaaat Ssssspooooooo..." He screwed up his eyes, trying to focus, to work out where he'd heard it before. The tiny blob of metal twitched, its minute legs cycling in the air. Its shiny wings flapped once, feebly, then with a last whirr, it stilled.

Wasp, Bill thought, his mind swimming as it got harder and harder to breathe. Wasp. Spy. Antelope. Not a spy. *Antelope. Not really a spy.*

Bill forced his eyes open. The antelope drew its head back, and winked. Then, with a click of its hooves, it set off at a run. Bill heard a long, loud noise sounding across the museum, echoing through the cases, setting the glass humming. He thought at first it was Whistler, whistling out one last breath, but as it built, he could make out the sound.

"Eeeeeeeeeeeeeeeeeeeeeeeeeeeeeeeeeeeeeeeeeeeeeeef!"

With a sudden clatter of hooves, the antelope sailed through the air, and smashed into the glass front of the Ripening case. The glass shattered instantly, showering the floor with tiny fragments, and the antelope dropped like a stone among the shards, utterly still. Rabbity creatures began to hop out across the floor. Graham gingerly stepped forward, sniffing the air. Above his head, a small dark butterfly flew jerkily out into the room.

Bill blinked fuzzily at the butterfly, and saw a row of iridescent spots running along the edges of its wings. Not bad, for the last thing he'd ever see, he thought dizzily, letting his head droop forward.

"Noooo!" howled the Great Spondozo. "Not the Pearl Bordered Fritillary! Guards, catch it! Forget them! Catch it at once!"

Bill felt the iron grip around his neck slacken, and he fell numbly to the floor as the Gatherers strode away, their huge gloves swatting at the air.

"It was only at the chrysalis stage last time I looked!" wailed Spondozo, wringing her gnarled hands. "It's the only one left, the only one in all the worlds! Everything else is replaceable, but... but... Oh, come here, you horrible flapping thing!" She began flailing her arms in the air, strings of grey hair escaping from her bun.

The Pearl Bordered Fritillary swooped crookedly away from her, and fluttered around the pale globe of light in the centre of the room. The Gatherers went on marching after it, their hands raised up, oblivious to the fact that it was out of reach.

Bill rose awkwardly to his knees, cradling his bitten hand. Some distance away, he could see Whistler crouching beside Antenmann, trying to pull the old alien out of the path of the Gatherers' boots. Close by was a ragged looking Tallulah, her dirty face streaked with tears. In her hands she held a tattered scrap of green cloth.

"Oh, no," Bill whispered, as the princess turned her brimming eyes to his. "No, it can't be..."

Bill shut his eyes. Then he shivered, as a low, fluting music lifted into the air. The song had no words, but there was a pattern in it, a refrain that repeated over and over, running up and down through the same few notes, with a knocking sound beneath it keeping the rhythm. Bill twisted round, trying to work out where it was coming from. The knocking grew louder, the music rising higher, and from within the press of Gatherers came Antenmann's chair, stomping out the rhythm with its rocking, lurching steps. Swaying in the seat, her little hands clinging to the carved wooden arms, was Phly. Her cloak was gone, and what was left of her flowing gown was ragged and torn, but her big dark eyes were shining as she sang.

The chair stumped its way across the museum's curving floor, and as it halted, the haunting melody died away.

"My word," wheezed Antenmann. "Try putting *that* in a glass box."

Phly smiled bashfully, then raised a slender hand into the air. Resting on her finger like a living jewelled ring was the Pearl Bordered Fritillary.

"My butterfly!" croaked the Great Spondozo, pushing her way impatiently past the Gatherers, her cardigan snagging on their huge elbows. "Give it to me! I want it!"

Phly opened her mouth, and hummed out a few bars of her song. The butterfly flapped its wings and rose into the air, darting just above the old woman's head.

"Guards!" shrieked Spondozo, grabbing at the fluttering creature. "Guards, help me!"

To Bill's astonishment, Tallulah suddenly sprinted forwards, as if she planned to take on the entire Gatherer army single-handed. At the last moment, she seemed to lose her footing, and skidded onto the floor before their feet. The Gatherers began to move slowly forwards, their heavy black boots rising to crush her, and Bill opened his mouth to scream a warning, but before they could take another step the princess had flung herself beneath their feet, and seized upon a small, black box lying abandoned on the floor. She brought her hand down on it, hard, and Bill caught a glimpse of a crooked grin as she curled into a ball, and rolled out of their way.

The Gatherers kept going, but there was something oddly uncoordinated about their movements. Their steps were jerky. Some of them began to walk in a different direction from the others. One spun around, and walked straight into the nearest display cabinet, scattering more broken glass across the floor; another bumped into it, and sent them both tumbling into the case, on top of a large pile of mouldy-looking carpets.

"Come here!" screeched Spondozo again, oblivious, still flailing her arms as the butterfly fluttered on through the museum, hovering just out of reach.

Bill scrambled out of the way as an out of control Gatherer lurched towards him, arms outstretched. It staggered past, and toppled head-first through one of the open doorways in the floor. Tallulah whooped with delight, and Bill caught a glimpse of the antelope trotting at her feet as she dashed about in the middle of the randomly wandering guards. She grabbed hold of one stumbling figure, and turned it around, giving it a push and giggling as it collided with another. Phly began stomping across the room, following the flight of the butterfly and letting Antenmann's chair knock aside any Gatherers who got in her way.

Bill felt the antelope brush past his leg as the Great Spondozo let out a shout of glee. The Pearl Bordered Fritillary had apparently grown tired of its haphazard flight, and had settled on the floor of the old woman's personal display case, its pearly white spots standing out against the red plush.

"I've got you now, you nasty little insect!" cried Spondozo, stepping into the case, and grasping the butterfly in both hands. As she turned to declare her victory, the antelope nudged the door closed with its head, and slid the lever home.

The Great Spondozo opened her cupped hands to free herself, letting the Pearl Bordered Fritillary flutter into the air, but it was too late. With a humming sound, purple light flooded down upon them, and fixed them in time. Spondozo was frozen with her mouth open, her hair straggling around a face twisted with fury. The butterfly, caught in the same numbing beam of light, stilled its wings, and, after lingering in the air for a tantalising moment, dropped onto the plush like an apple from a tree. The purple beam faded, and the glass case went dim.

As the light went out, across the museum there was a huge clanking clatter, as the malfunctioning Gatherer army toppled as one to the floor.

"Woohoo!" yelled Tallulah, giving one of them a celebratory kick in the head, and kissing the squat black box of the Great Spondozo's Deactivator.

Phly hopped down from the chair, and tinkled with joy as Whistler swept her up into a hug. Bill smiled, sank weakly onto the floor before Spondozo's case, and gave the antelope a grateful stroke on the nose.

The antelope blinked at him. Bill blinked back. There was a white patch on its left ear that he'd never noticed before. Its horns seemed to have grown longer, too.

There was a tapping sound behind him, and he felt something warm, wet and slightly scratchy on his skin.

The antelope was licking his injured hand. *Another* antelope.

There was more tapping, and a series of gentle 'eef'ing noises behind him.

"I say, chaps," announced a plummy voice. Bill turned to see Graham standing in the midst of a vast herd of chocolatey-eyed, pointy-horned, long-eared creatures. "Is it just me, or is there an awfully large number of antelopes in here?"

Chapter Fifteen

The Perfect AND

… in which there are two boys,
and an awful lot of antelopes

"Blimey," whispered Bill, gawping at the sight of several hundred antelopes trotting delicately between the still bodies of the Gatherers, spilling out of the round wooden doors, beside him, above him, all around him.

"Graham!" pealed Phly, skipping through the herd in a ragged green blur, and flinging her arms around the tall boy's leg. He scooped her up in his arms, and beamed.

"Hello, old thing!" he said, setting his peaked cap on her little head and making her giggle. "Hello, Captain. Greetings, your majesty. I don't mind saying, it's jolly nice to see you all again. Quite an adventure, eh?"

"Adventure, yes," said Whistler, absently shaking Graham's hand as he stared at the antelopes. "Of course, it's all in a day's work, for a… well…"

"And you must be Bill," said Graham, striding through the herd. He pumped Bill's hand in a vigorous handshake, smiling and showing off his bright white teeth. "Super to make your acquaintance. I trust you've been looking after these friends of mine?"

Bill nodded politely. He suddenly felt very young, very pale, and even shorter than usual.

"I've been having a simply ripping time," Graham went on. "Lashings of excitement, plenty of derring-do. Defeating evil and all that. This is the life for chaps like us, eh, Bill?"

Bill looked up at the tall, tanned boy, and had a terrible feeling that somewhere, some time ago, there had been a terrible mistake, and that he, Bill, had somehow ended up on someone else's adventure.

"It appears we had some help," said Whistler, still mesmerized by the antelopes.

"Just a little bit," said Tallulah, stumbling as they wove around her legs. "Where are they all coming from? And more to the point, why? That pilfing 'lope stiffed us."

"It didn't mean to," said Bill, scanning the herd anxiously. "When we were in the delegates' rooms on Quxyng, there was a wasp trying to zap me, just like they zapped you. When we left the room…"

"You mean when we were chasing you down the corridor trying to murder you?" said Tallulah.

"Um… yeah," said Bill, coughing a little as Graham shot him a dubious look. "Well, it must've zapped the antelope instead. When the wasp fell out, it was all right again. And then it smashed the glass, and set the butterfly free. It saved us."

He went on searching through the herd, trying to sort antelope from antelope, remembering how still the little creature had lain among the glittering shards. Then there was a low 'eef'ing, a rhythmic pattering of hooves, and the teeming herd parted. Standing rather unsteadily, with sparkling splinters of glass freckling its back, was the antelope: their antelope.

It blinked.

"Clever 'lope!" sang Phly, hopping out of Graham's arms to give it a hug. Bill moved to join them, but Graham got there first, brushing the glass away with a broad hand, and fondly ruffling the antelope's long ears.

There was an uneven thumping sound, and Bill looked up to see Antenmann, back in his chair, stumping towards them.

"I think you'll find they're all rather clever," he rasped. "I believe these creatures have been planning something like this for some time."

Whistler's gills hummed faintly. "The rumours," he murmured, "they were true. This is the resistance. This is the secret underground movement who were fighting back against the Great Spondozo."

The antelope performed a small tap-dance.

"Ever so clever 'lope!" sang Phly, giving it an even tighter hug. "Tell us, lovely creature, how did you get so clever? And where did you all come from? And how did you…"

Tallulah cleared her throat pointedly. "Oi! Phly!" she said. "I reckon we've covered this, but I don't mind saying it again: the antelope *can't talk*."

Hundreds of chocolatey eyes turned her way, and blinked.

"I mean," said the princess, looking a little disconcerted, "well, maybe it's a bit smarter than I was giving it credit for."

"Eef," said the antelope. The other antelopes blinked again. Bill narrowed his eyes, and wondered.

"I believe Adelaide discovered they were plotting against her some decades ago," rasped Antenmann. "There always seemed to be rather a lot of them in the dungeons."

"And you just left them there?" said Tallulah, looking sourly at the old Quxynggrotly.

"Indeed," Antenmann said. "I was fairly certain they were allowing themselves to be captured on purpose: building a hidden army, right under her nose, just waiting for an opportunity such as this to strike. Besides which, I try not to involve myself in politics. I had other very important work to occupy my time."

"Like building the Gatherers?" said Whistler, in a reproachful tone.

"Yes, well," said the old alien, the feet of his chair shuffling awkwardly. "Down here at the centre of the universe, it's really rather difficult to know what's going on out there. It wasn't my choice to put them to that use. And I did build the Deactivator," he added, hopefully.

Bill tentatively wiggled the fingers of his sore hand, wincing.

"Just not the one that worked," said Tallulah.

"Well, now, I didn't know that," croaked Antenmann. "And I was willing to sacrifice them. Once I realized what you had in that Knowletron… it's all I've ever wanted."

Whistler stared at Antenmann, his gills quivering faintly.

"Congratulations," croaked the ancient explorer, with a wistful smile. "You did what I could not. You completed the map."

With a trembling, damp hand, Whistler reached into his dungarees, and pulled out the square of silver. His mouth opened and closed a few times as he gazed at it, but no sound came out.

"All I ever wanted," Antenmann repeated, in a whisper. "The Perfect AND, and the perfect map. But the havoc it would have unleashed, in her hands… I couldn't let that happen…"

"What do you want, a medal?" grunted Tallulah. "You should count yourself lucky we didn't shove you into that box with the old bat."

Phly gave a soft little hum, and pushed through the antelopes to the Great Spondozo's display case. She pressed her nose against the glass.

"Poor butterfly," she sang. "Can we let the others out, now?"

Tallulah's smudged face broke into a broad grin. "*Now* you're talking," she said, turning to face a cabinet crammed with oddly-shaped musical instruments, and stiff, lifeless figures frozen as if playing them. "And I reckon that 'lope knew just how to do it."

She took a few steps back, then, taking a deep breath, ran towards the glass case, yelling a long, loud, "*Eeeeeeeeeef!*" as she ran. At last moment she twisted, and raised her feet into the air, smashing her heavy black boots into the glass and shattering it into thousands of pieces.

As she picked herself up off the floor, the frozen

figures within began to stir; awkwardly at first, their lungs unused to breathing, their fingers cold and creaking. But as the life began to flow back to them, their taut faces relaxed into smiles, and their glassy eyes began to shine.

All around the museum, the cry of "Eeeeeeef!" rang out, and suddenly glass was flying everywhere, as the hordes of antelopes hurled themselves into the display cases. The sound of breaking glass became mingled with talking, and shouts of laughter, as the freed exhibits summoned up their rusty voices. Figures who had stood for decades side by side could at last turn and speak. Weary limbs could at last be rested. Their delight, and gratitude, was quite overwhelming, and Bill found himself engulfed in embraces, and handshakes, and an odd ear-stroking ritual that a series of three-eyed hairy creatures insisted on performing. He could see Phly being carried around on people's shoulders, squealing with glee. He spotted Tallulah poking through the shattered glass around a case filled with crumpled scrolls of paper and cooking pots; she suddenly grinned, and ripped a sheet out from a thick, stained old book, stuffing it into her pocket. Graham was clapping people heartily on the back and directing them out through the round doors. Whistler and Antenmann seemed to have disappeared, presumably down to the dungeons to free the prisoners; most of the antelopes seemed to have followed them. Gradually, the throng of elated ex-exhibits began to thin out.

Bill heard the bellowing voice of the rust-red knight directing people to the Gatherer ships from somewhere below. There were sweet, fluting voices singing a song called 'Why We Love Butterflies', accompanied by an odd twanging sound. Slowly, the voices faded, and the smashing sounds died away. Exhausted, Bill gazed round what was left of the Big Museum of Things. The floor was ankle-deep in broken glass. Scattered bits of cloth, and paper, and rusty bits of machinery lay discarded in small heaps on the floor, mingling with the fallen bodies of the Gatherers. The only thing left standing was the Great Spondozo's display case, her frozen, angry stare somehow all the more frightening for its loneliness.

Graham appeared by Bill's side, wiping sweat off his brow, and grinning.

"I say, Bill, this is all rather jolly, don't you think?" he said, punching Bill's shoulder playfully, and sending him stumbling sideways.

Bill coughed, wondering what to say, but before he could speak, a scraping sound made them both turn.

Whistler and Antenmann, with some considerable help from his chair, were pushing something huge out of one of the round doors in the floor. It was draped in musty, tattered cloth, but the curvy shape, with odd bits sticking out of the back, was unmistakeable.

"The Brian IV!" announced Whistler breathlessly, whipping away the cloth to reveal Antenmann's famous rocket. It had been given a good polish all over, and was now almost gleaming.

"Restored to its former glory," he said proudly, "with one addition: the universe's first Perfect AND."

Climbing up onto the rocket, and twisting the stiff handle, Whistler hefted the hatch open. Resting on the AND was the Knowletron, its globe of light glowing brightly.

"Pilf," murmured Tallulah, giving Bill's elbow a nudge.

He looked round, and saw that the pale globe of light hanging in the centre of the museum was now glowing too. Within its sphere, wiry golden hoops appeared, all spinning and revolving, keeping their central point and never stilling for a moment; the hoops radiated out from the centre, each larger than the last by a fraction, never overlapping but revolving separately, perfectly, inside one another. As the hoops spun round, they sparked, tiny points of light flaring at intervals all through the globe.

"It's true," Whistler said, his voice trembling. "I did it. I completed the map. This ship can take you anywhere, anywhere you want to go, in a matter of moments. This ship can take you *home*." He looked at Bill and Graham. "*All* of you."

"Hooray!" trilled Phly, spinning round and round with her ragged robes swooping out around her.

"Can it take me somewhere else?" said Tallulah. "I think I've been hugged to death enough for one day."

"Home?" said Graham, guffawing loudly. "When there are adventures to have? Evil villains to defeat? I don't think we're quite ready for the humdrum life, eh, Bill?"

Bill bit his lip, and cleared his throat awkwardly. "Um... actually I'd quite like to go home."

Graham stared at him.

"Not that I haven't enjoyed myself," Bill added quickly, looking round at Whistler, and Tallulah, and Phly, and the antelope. "It's been very... interesting. But I think my parents would probably like to know where I am. My hand hurts a bit. And… well, I'd quite like to sleep in my own bed tonight."

"Oh, thank goodness!" wailed Graham, suddenly sagging into Bill's arms and sobbing. "I hate it here! I fell down that ghastly hole, into that vile dungeon, and then they put me in here. I haven't had any adventures at all!"

Bill stared down at the weeping figure in amazement, as Graham clutched a chunk of Bill's scarf and noisily blew his nose on it. "Please," he moaned, "take me home. I want my mummy."

"We have our first destination," said Whistler with a smile, reaching out a bony grey hand. "Step aboard, we depart immediately."

The antelope 'eef'ed, and gracefully hopped up through the hatch at once. Tallulah and Bill paused at the hatchway, and looked out across the wreckage of the museum, at the single, unbroken glass case, with its one, glassy-eyed inhabitant, and the tiny, frozen butterfly by her foot.

"Don't worry," rasped a voice from below. "I'll keep an eye on her."

"Aren't you coming with us?" sang Phly, poking her nose out of the hatch.

Antenmann shook his wizened head. "I think I've earned the role of her guardian," he croaked. "Just as others have earned theirs."

The ancient Quxynggrotly seemed to straighten himself up in his chair, and Bill saw Whistler gazing down at Antenmann from inside the ship, a solemn look on his face. Antenmann's skeletal finger stroked the silver surface of the Brian IV one last time, and Whistler nodded, silently.

"Besides," Antenmann went on, wrinkling his wrinkles into a smile, "after all those centuries building the dratted thing, I'd like to be here to watch this AND work properly for the very first time."

Tallulah frowned. "You mean, it's never been tested?"

"Oh, no," said Antenmann, rasping out a chuckle. "Totally experimental. My newly modified AND works on a new principle, and it's never been used with a map of this size before. A machine that can make every layer of the universe rotate against its axis, and line up with the one beneath? The possible disastrous consequences of such a phenomenal act are too vast to even contemplate: temporal flux, gravitational collapse…"

He paused, and chuckled again at her expression. "That's the joy of science, my dear. You never know what might go wrong until you try."

With a twinkly smile, he waited for them to climb aboard, slid the hatch into place, and with a clang sealed it shut.

"Bye-bye!" hummed Phly, her small hand gripping Bill's finger tightly.

"Don't wait up," called Tallulah, grinning.

Bill wriggled uncomfortably: it was extremely cramped with so many of them in there, especially as Graham seemed to have taken a liking to him after his confession, and insisted on sitting on his lap. Graham sniffed loudly on Bill's shoulder, and the antelope gave him a stern, slightly scathing blink.

Whistler beamed at them all, then ran a bony hand over the ship's controls.

"Prepare for take off," he said, breathless with anticipation.

Bill took a last look at the confines of the tiny ship, and closed his eyes.

With a mighty roar, the Brian IV took them home.

Epilogue

The End

… in which this story ends

Geography was not Bill's favourite subject. The South Wales coast was familiar enough from behind the weatherman on television, and he knew the shapes of America and Australia and Africa, although he got muddled over where one continent ended and the next began. But most of the rest just looked like differently coloured blobs, and he'd always felt it was a good thing that a large part of his world was covered in sea, so you didn't have to learn any of it.

As Bill and Graham climbed down from the hatch of the Brian IV to a chorus of goodbyes, Bill felt immensely relieved to hear the crashing of waves, and to smell the familiar salt air.

"Cripes!" said Graham loudly in Bill's ear, as the rocket fired its engines, and shot away again in a flash. "Where the devil do you suppose we are?"

Bill looked down and saw sand beneath his feet. He looked up, and saw foaming crystal waves, lapping at a nearby shore. He turned in a circle, and saw more waves, on every side, sparkling in the hot sunshine. A few feet from his leg was a single palm tree.

However bad Bill was at Geography, Whistler was apparently worse.

He was just opening his mouth to say so, when Graham was hit on the head by a falling coconut, and slumped into his arms. As Bill fell backwards, he caught a glimpse out of the corner of his eye of a large black hole opening up in the sand, and swallowing him.

And then they just fell...

And fell...

And fell...

Until they hit the bottom.

But that's quite another story.